GLINT OF GOLD

GLINT OF GOLD

Frances Paige

This first world edition published in Great Britain 2006 by
SEVERN HOUSE PUBLISHERS LTD of
9–15 High Street, Sutton, Surrey SM1 1DF.
This first world edition published in the USA 2006 by
SEVERN HOUSE PUBLISHERS INC of
595 Madison Avenue, New York, N.Y. 10022.

British Library Cataloguing in Publication Data

Paige,   Frances
    Glint of Gold
    1.   Hotelkeepers - France - Dordogne (France) - Fiction
    2.   Dordogne (France) - Fiction
    3.   Love stories
    I.   Title
    823.9'14 [F]

    ISBN-10: 0-7278-6347-9

Typeset by Palimpsest Book Production Ltd.,
Polmont, Stirlingshire, Scotland.
Printed and bound in Great Britain by
MPG Books Ltd., Bodmin, Cornwall.

For Helen, my daughter, who loves France.

One

Merle and I were Francophiles. It still hurts to look back on those golden days of the sixties and seventies, when we took off for France once the daffodils were over and the children were back at school, generally about May. We didn't fly as most people do nowadays, but motored from our village in Kent to Dover, and drove on to the cross-channel ferry. The excitement when we reached Calais, as we took in our first breaths of the French air, a heady mixture of crustaceans and Gauloises!

But we longed to feel the heat of the sun on our covered-up wintered bodies, and so off we set for the south in search of it, stopping en route at various small hotels on the way. These stop-overs would make a travel book on their own – indeed they have, because I'm a travel writer, and I have encapsulated them in several books extolling their appeal. The best ones, of course, we have kept to ourselves, especially the one which we stopped at in 1966, in the south-west, that land of rivers and castles, Freda White land.

We had detoured on this particular occasion and we found ourselves in Souillac, on the Dordogne, where we stopped. It was bustling with traffic, being on the N20 route to Spain, and we craved the peace and quiet of a little village. However, we owed it to Souillac to look round it, especially at the splendid church with its statue of Isaiah, and to browse amongst the little shops in the side streets, finishing with tea and patisseries in a *salon de thé*, watching the traffic. I took a schoolboy delight in those establishments with their hot water jugs and teapots, their lemon slices, their paper napkins and silver forks, or perhaps it was the memory of sinking my teeth into a chocolate eclair or a strawberry tartlet.

1

We drove along by the river, and eventually there it was, what we were looking for, a picture-book village with all the necessary requisites, the ornate gates of the local château, the post office cum village shop, the baker's, an hotel, a long low building in the *place*, with window-boxes of petunias, and ivy covering its front. 'Le Tilleul', we could just read its name above the door. There were tables and chairs set around a lime tree growing in the middle of the square, obviously giving the hotel its name. As we parked, a shepherd with his *troupeau* trailed slowly past us. He raised a hand in greeting, the bells round the sheeps' necks tinkled, and to crown it all, the little cavalcade was bathed in a rosy pink from the setting sun. We looked at each other. This is it, we said.

We pushed open the swing door into a large pleasant dining room with beamed ceiling, a bar at one end and a huge stone fireplace at the other. We found out later that they roasted *sanglier*, wild boar, during the hunting season. There was a youngish dark-haired man at the bar, and he raised his head, smiling, 'M'sieu, Madame?' Yes, fortunately, he said, in answer to our enquiry, there was a room vacant.

He had a pleasant manner. Merle, though shy of strangers in general, relaxed quickly under his friendliness, and soon they were getting on like a house on fire. 'My wife will show you upstairs,' he said. 'You will be in room five, I will tell her.' He called to a young woman who was laying tables, 'Marie! Are you busy? *Numero cinq, s'il te plaît.*' I thought his bearing was rather deferential, given she was his wife. Merle always said I was sensitive to atmosphere and nuances, but the woman was pleasant enough to us as she led us upstairs to a room overlooking the *tilleul* tree and the *place*.

We chatted with her for a few minutes, and when I asked her what were the attractions of the village, she seemed to brighten, talking about the good walks there were, and the views one could get from the *causse* – here she waved her hand, and when we looked blank she explained that the *causse* was the high upland behind the village, bare limestone plateaux that could be found throughout the centre and south of France. Then there was the river, *naturellement*. 'Henri spends a lot of his time there, fishing . . .' She shrugged her shoulders, her mouth turned down, and she spoke in a quiet, rapid French to Merle.

When she had gone I said to Merle, 'Was she venting her spleen on her husband?'

'In a way,' she said. 'Women's talk, implying that we all had grudges against our husbands. How they never considered us, left us alone while they went off to enjoy themselves.'

'I don't do that, do I?' I teased her.

'Well, you work at home,' she said. 'I can keep tabs on you.' She smiled as she said this; Merle was committed to being a good wife, and would never have dreamed of declaring grudges against me in public.

'They can do that with each other,' I pointed out.

I don't know why I remember this conversation. Well, yes, I do. It has some bearing on what was to follow.

After we had freshened up, we went downstairs and out to the tables round the lime tree where the husband was officiating, now wearing a white jacket and black bow tie. When I asked him what he recommended to drink, he said he had a white wine that was a favourite with his customers, a Gaillac Perlé. I said OK, and he brought a bottle wrapped in a white napkin to our table. 'Not quite local,' he said, 'but superb.' It was ice cold and delicious. When we agreed with him after our first sip, he nodded, filled our glasses and said that unfortunately, it didn't travel well. We later found out in England that this was true: when dining out one night we tried to recapture the joy of that stay in Bernay, as the village was called, by ordering a bottle. It hadn't the sparkle of the Bernay Gaillac. I remember that night because we were so happy. It was before . . . but back to my story, my therapy, which I haven't felt able to try out on myself until now.

There was a fair-haired, youngish man sitting alone at the table next to us. I met his eyes over my glass, and he nodded. 'Yes,' he said, 'it's a good wine that. But Henri is right. It doesn't travel well.'

'Are you a connoisseur of local wines?' I asked him.

He shook his head. 'No, only of birds. I'm an engineer,

3

and I'm combining an inspection of a water tower here with seeing what the bird life's like.'

'My husband is a bit of an ornithologist,' Merle smiled at the man. He raised his eyebrows at me.

'True,' I said. 'Why not join us and we can talk about birds?'

He was good company. He told us he was from Alsace, hence his fair colouring, I supposed, and that the bird he was particularly interested in was the golden oriole, sometimes seen in these parts.

'Have you been lucky?' I asked him. He smiled in a peculiar way.

'Yes,' he said, 'in more ways than one.' He gave me a man-to-man look, and I was puzzled. What was he getting at? I was trying to figure him out. He wore a rough workman's shirt and corduroy trousers, but his hands were well cared for. He had an ease of manner, especially with Merle, a closed, smiling face – that is, he didn't show his teeth, but his mouth had a one-sided upward tilt to it, and there were good-humoured lines round his eyes. He was slimly built. He was definitely not the usual French workman.

'Does the hotel here depend on the tower for water?' I asked him. We had noticed its rearing shape in a field behind the hotel.

He said it did. 'Marie told me the English were the worst for complaining if the supply failed.' He laughed. 'Poor Henri! He had to carry water up by the bucketful to fill the bath of an Englishwoman. She insisted.'

Again I thought his manner was strange. 'Not very funny for Monsieur,' Merle said, and I knew she was on my wavelength.

'You seem to know the hotel owners very well,' I said. 'Are you staying here?'

'No,' he said. 'I'm sharing a flat in Souillac with a colleague while we quarter this district, looking at the water towers.'

The other guests were rising from their seats and going into the dining room. 'I think dinner is being served,' Merle said.

'You're welcome to join us, Monsieur.' I got up.

4

Again the one-sided smile, 'You're very kind, but no, thank you. I have to get back to Souillac. Paper work, you know.' The smile seemed to indicate much more than the words. We were both on our feet. 'Perhaps you would like to join me sometime, Monsieur, in searching for the golden oriole?' he said.

I thanked him, but he didn't suggest a date and nor did I. We said goodbye, and I followed Merle.

'Very handsome,' she said while we were doing justice to the excellent venison pâté we had been served with. 'Did you notice the golden glint in his hair?'

'No, I'm not as susceptible as you, darling.'

'Oh,' she said, 'but I didn't like him. I thought him . . . fishy.'

'Did you?'

'Shall you go birdwatching with him?'

'No, I prefer to do that on my own.' I always travelled with my bird books. Merle's interest was in the flora and fauna so we were both happy.

We liked the atmosphere of the village so much that we stayed more than a week of our holiday. The surrounding walks were good, and, advised by Henri, who became a friend as well as an informant, we made several discoveries which endeared us to the place, like la Source Bleu, a pool nearby reached by pushing through a maze of thickets in a wood near the village. It certainly looked blue, which was puzzling because the sky was hidden by the overhanging trees, and there couldn't possibly be any reflection from it. It had a peculiar attraction for us because of its unexplainable colour, and the silence. 'Eerie,' Merle said. 'Typical of this place.'

I agreed. 'No sound of birds.'

He also directed us to the *causse* that his wife had mentioned. We took a path behind the church; it was more like a tunnel, in fact, because of the trees on either side, and again there was the silence which we had noticed at the blue pool, a vast silence, as if we were in touch with nature, and were the only inhabitants of the world.

We never met anyone there, but we were both entranced

by the wild flowers, eglantine and honeysuckle entwined in the hedges, and underneath, wild sweet peas, vetch and lavender. In France, nature is more prolific in May than at home. Merle exclaimed at the varieties of orchids she found, and I kept a lookout for a glint of gold which might be the golden oriole.

The *causse* was a revelation when we reached it, a vast expanse of close-cropped grass, miles and miles of it, and in the distance beyond, a landscape of rolling fields, with trees and red-roofed farms tucked in the folds, all backed by the blue shadow of the Auvergne.

The short grass was an enticement, and we spent many hours lying there, the smell of wild thyme in our nostrils, watching the swifts swooping and darting above us. We had to choose our bed carefully, because of the outcrops of limestone. Once, when we were resting there, we heard the tinkle of bells, and a boy with a flock of goats passed us. His cheerful 'M'sieu, 'dame' amused us, because it was like a casual encounter in a busy street.

We visited caves, because, of course, it was cave country. After graduation I had spent a year in France teaching at Figeac, which was south-east of Souillac near the Lot, and had visited many caves at that time. Limestone is porous, Henri told us, and that we should look out for *avens* on the *causse*. I knew these holes in the ground were made by the rain running through the soil, hence the formation of underground rivers in some of the caves. 'There's another world down there,' he said. 'In some caves you can sail in a boat on a river, in other ones you can see marvellous paintings on the walls.' He inspired us to explore several in the surrounding district, especially the smaller, unknown ones, where, crawling behind the hired guide, we would be drenched in waves of garlic when he turned his head to speak to us. We had probably disturbed him at his meal. In those days a man in the village kept the key to allow one entry; nowadays, most of the caves are *'amenagée'*, managed. We made trips to the big ones, Padirac and La Cave, and there we would travel in boats on the underground rivers, or by train, while at Pech Merle we both marvelled at the wall

6

paintings that sprang to life when the guide shone his torch on them. 'The same eeriness,' Merle said, and I knew what she meant. The land above seemed to have borrowed some of the silence of the caves.

We studied books bought on our sorties to Souillac, and became aficionados of Edouard Martel and Abbé Breuil, but remained faithful to Bernay, and liked nothing better than strolling about the village, saluting the villagers, or sitting with a glass of wine at a table under the lime tree, and best of all, making our way to the *causse* through the tunnelled path for our daily walk. We wondered about the château as we saw, one day, a dark-haired woman driving through the open gates. There were two children in the back.

When we asked Henri about the owners, he said the château belonged to the Bernay family, that the old people had died, and Madame Gibert owned it now, their daughter, a divorcée, who lived in Paris and only came occasionally. 'I used to work there,' he told us, 'my cottage and the one adjoining belongs to the château. I and Monsieur Maury, an old man now, rent them.'

Once, about a week after our arrival, I was walking past the side of the hotel, Merle was resting in our room, when I saw Henri sitting on a straight-backed kitchen chair placed against the stone wall of his cottage. The long shadow of the water tower in the field behind stretched across the gravel. A rangy pup lay in it.

'Nice to see you without the *papillon,* Henri,' I said, referring to his usual black bow tie that he wore with an immaculate white jacket. He looked much younger.

'It's a relief,' he said.

'Madame resting?'

'Yes, it's a long day.'

'Hardly any water upstairs. I managed a trickle for my shower. I'm not complaining.'

'Some do,' he said, making a tutting sound with his tongue. 'But fortunately, she's left. Madame Elliott-Gregg. The one with the dog.'

'Yes, I remember. Merle offered to get water for that bad-tempered Scottie of hers from our room. She hardly thanked her.' I smiled, but decided to change the subject, thinking that water, or the shortage of it, was dangerous ground. 'I believe you fish,' I said. 'I remember Madame telling us.'

'Yes, I do,' he said, 'but it seems to have lost its appeal for me recently.' He brightened. 'Would you like me to take you with me if I go?'

'I'd love it. Could my wife come too? She's captivated by the countryside around here.'

'*Bien sûr*. What about tomorrow? It's time I got back to it.' He seemed to be cheered by the idea, and I agreed. We arranged to meet at four o'clock. Robert, the youth, who helped at the tables, would look after the bar while we were away, since Madame would be resting.

I set off along the village street thinking that Mrs Elliott-Gregg was the type who gave the English a bad name in France with her loud-mouthed demanding ways, the worst kind of ambassadress.

I loved my afternoon walks through the village. The priest would be working in his garden, his cassock hitched up, and there was the fresh smell of bread in the air from the shop next to his house. The children in their pinafores were straggling home from school, and women were gossiping at their doors. All of them greeted me cheerfully as if I were one of them. I stopped to speak to the joiners who worked in a disused garage, a cheerful bunch who turned out work of such precision and artistry that I would have willingly employed them at our cottage back home, indeed I had considered suggesting to Guy, their boss, such an idea. Possibly the joiners in England had had such skills before the advent of the DIY stores.

When I told Merle that Henri was taking us fishing the following day, her face lit up. 'Great!' she said. 'I love this place, Martin. It's cast its spell on me. I feel something's telling me to enjoy it while I can. Do you get it too?'

I said I felt something of the same. 'How about looking out for a house here? I'm sure Henri could help us, and we could ask Guy Rosier to do the joinery. When I get home I'll work like the very devil to make money for it.'

We laughed, but I felt I had made a solemn pact. Yet in

spite of our happiness, a dread hung over me, as if something would spoil our plans. I told myself I was being fanciful.

Henri was waiting for us in his car at the corner of his house. He greeted us cheerfully, and told us to climb in the back. His pup, a rangy kind of hound with droopy ears and a doleful expression, was sitting in the passenger seat. 'Papillon monopolizes the front,' he said.

He drove us away from the village, towards Souillac. The road was lined with trees, and there was the occasional farmhouse and flocks of sheep in the fields, but apart from an old woman sitting knitting while her goats grazed round her, we never saw a soul. He turned off the road after two or three miles, and drove down a bumpy track that I thought must be wreaking havoc on his springs and tyres, but he didn't seem to mind and patted Papillon while he drove. '*Ne vous inquiétez pas*,' he shouted to us, telling us not to worry. We were all laughing when he eventually drew up at a ruined mill by the side of the river. When we got out, I was aware of the sound of the mill race breaking the silence. There was a stone bridge over the river, and I had the feeling I had stepped through the frame into the heart of a picture. Merle said in English to me, 'You're the one for atmosphere. Do you feel it here?'

I nodded.

Although Henri couldn't understand our exchange, he said, 'Quiet, isn't it? No one comes down here now. They say it's haunted. The miller and his wife who used to live here had a daughter, and she drowned in the river. Such a tragedy. After it happened, people used to come down out of curiosity. Some said the strands of green weed in the river looked like her hair.' Merle, who had been poking about the place, reappeared. She looked pale.

'Anything wrong?' I asked her.

'There are blankets inside on a makeshift bed.'

'Possibly a tramp has been sleeping there,' I said.

Henri, who had looked uncomprehending, said, 'Anyhow, it makes it nice and quiet for me. Even fishermen don't like it because their wives won't cook the fish they catch here. I give it to our guests and they don't complain.' He laughed.

'If you catch any,' Merle said, 'don't give them to us. Promise?'

'Promise,' he said. He led us round behind the mill where he had a boat hidden in a little bay of the river, and invited us to get in. This we did, then he pushed it off from the bank, jumping in at the same time, and taking up one of the oars to guide us under the stone bridge.

We drifted with the tide down the smooth river, the surface the colour of bottle glass because of the overhanging trees. It was very quiet, and when a jay called loudly, it startled us. Henri was knowledgeable about birds. He identified them to us, woodpeckers, jays and once a hoopoe. But it was Merle who spotted the heron at the edge of the river. Our voices startled it, because it flapped its wings and flew awkwardly off, probably annoyed that its peace had been disturbed.

'Have you seen any golden orioles around here?' I asked him, and he shook his head.

'They're shy birds. You'll be lucky.'

'The water tower inspector claims to have seen them. You know who I mean?'

'He was here when you arrived. He doesn't stay, though.' He was terse.

'Yes, we had a drink with him,' I said. 'He comes from Alsace. You don't see many fair-haired people around here, do you?'

'No. He did ask for a room at the beginning, but I told him I had guests coming. I didn't like his manner.'

I nodded. 'I know what you mean.'

'Oh, how horrible!' Merle was shaking some weed from her hand which she had been trailing in the water. I noticed again how pale she looked.

'The maiden's hair,' Henri said. 'That's what they call it. Do not be alarmed, Madame. But I know you are sensible.' He smiled at her, and she smiled back.

'Generally I am, but the atmosphere here . . .' She laughed. 'When do we begin to fish, Henri?'

'Soon. I am making for my own special place. Ah, here it is.' We had rounded a bend in the river, and ahead there was a pool with a stone wall behind it, an ordinary stone wall, perhaps the remains of another ruin, except that, to our surprise, it was covered with small blue butterflies. Merle exclaimed with pleasure. 'I thought you would like them,' Henri said. 'The *causses bleus* seem to gather here. The wall gets heated by the sun, and it attracts them. Here we stop.' He provided me with a rod. Merle said she would rather watch the butterflies. He took up a rod from the bottom of the boat, and proceeded to bait his and mine.

The silence was deep and we stopped talking in case we scared the fish. The only noise was an occasional call from a bird, and I listened for the oriole. It has a loud fluid whistle, but I didn't hear it. My unease about the place had quite gone; Merle looked happy, her eyes on the wall, watching the butterflies. Where could I find such peace, I wondered, such quiet? It made our village in Kent seem positively noisy in comparison, with lawn mowers, people's voices and revving cars. Time passed. Henri and I caught two fish each, the butterflies had fluttered away, the setting sun failed to reach us, and it began to feel rather chilly.

'We'll have to get back for the evening meal,' Henri said. 'I'm the cook.' His voice sounded loud in the quietness, and we both agreed. 'But first,' he said, 'I have to show you my party piece.'

He steered the boat to the bank, told me to hold the oars, and clambered out without further explanation. Merle and I looked at each other, puzzled.

He stood looking at the stone wall, now bereft of butter-flies, then launched himself towards it. We exchanged glances again. The next thing we saw was his body flat against the wall, then him clambering up it, for all the world like the small lizards we often saw sunning themselves on the *causse*. I didn't know where he was finding the handholds or footholds (there were certainly outcrops of what looked like gorse), except that he went up the wall like a . . . lizard. He came down the same way and turned to us laughing, and bowed. 'I used to amuse Marie with that trick,' he said. His face seemed sad.

'Bravo!' I said, and we clapped our hands in applause. He came towards us and got into the boat.

The mill was in shadow when we got back to it, and I thought how it had once housed a man and his wife and young daughter. No one would want to live there now. Besides, it was difficult to get to; there was that road, but no doubt when the place had been inhabited, it had been kept clear. We stood and looked at the mill, while Henri tied up his boat. 'But he cheered us up by his performance,' Merle said, as if to convince herself.

When we got back to the car Papillon barked loudly to welcome us. He had been shut in by Henri, who had said the dog wasn't a good sailor.

'How do you know?' I asked him.

'I've tried him often. He refuses to pass the mill. Backs away, barking. I've lifted him and dumped him in the boat, but he jumps out and runs away and I have a devil of a job trying to catch him.'

We had pork for dinner that night, not fish. Henri was as good as his word.

We had a chat with the priest the following day. 'That ruined mill on the river,' I said. 'Will no one go near it?'

'No one in the village,' he said. 'I've even been asked to exorcize it. I've tried to talk them out of it, but haven't succeeded. Henri is the exception. He likes to fish there, although no one else does. But I'm the beneficiary.' He laughed jovially, his hands on his fat stomach.

Merle said she wouldn't like to go back again, but strangely enough, Henri never asked us.

I greeted him as I passed the following day. He was sitting on his usual chair. 'Off for my afternoon walk.' He nodded. He seemed morose. Was it a marital problem, I wondered. 'Marie is resting,' he said. 'She mustn't be disturbed. That is the rule.' I felt I was getting into deep water, and after a few words I set off on my walk through the village.

How lucky I was, I thought, with a wife like Merle. I promised myself I would take good care of her. 'The lass with the delicate air.' The words of an old Scottish song had come into my mind when I had first met her. She had looked pale on the expedition to the ruined mill, I thought.

I was determined to find the golden oriole. I had read

12

about it in the room before I started. 'Habitat essentially arboreal; well-timbered parks, old orchards, river banks, woods, seldom in the open.' I would make for the tunnelled path leading to the *causse*.

The profusion of flowers and butterflies in that path behind the church almost made me desert my search. Where in England, I thought, would you find such a variety of wild flowers? No wonder Merle had been enchanted. I knew that the path descended into a deeply-wooded declivity, and I had hopes of seeing an oriole there. We had always carried on to the *causse* on our walks, and never deviated. When I reached the bottom I decided to climb over the fence. I saw that the overhanging trees were mostly lime, faintly perfumed. I pulled a spray and walked slowly along, examining the corn-coloured florets, the tender green of the inner leaves like pale fingers against the darker ones, stuck it in the breast pocket of my shirt.

The going was rough, the remains of a path composed of a scattering of sharp pieces of flint that were sore on the feet, and I stopped for a rest and looked back at the village, the church perched on the brow of the hill, pantile-roofed cottages tucking themselves round it, the high water tower. The sky was a great bowl of china blue above it all.

I heard the tinny sound of the bells that the goats wore about their necks, and looking across the fields through a gap in the trees, I saw the hunched figure of someone sitting beside them. I waved to the red-jerseyed boy, and he waved back. Where in God's name, I thought, could you get a boy to sit on a lonely hillside for hours on end looking after goats?

Now the ground was running away rapidly under my feet, and it was getting darker. The path seemed to be sinking between the hedges, and there were no lime trees now, only heavy oak under which there were tangled growths of thorn, which together shut out the light. 'Habitat essentially arboreal.' Well, this was it all right. My feet were on mossy ground now, the path had disappeared. I was groping my way through fern and juniper, once or twice I tripped over limestone rocks jutting through the soil.

Somewhere, what sounded like a nightingale was singing, full-throated, which surprised me. 'A skulking solitary bird,' my book said. Try writing a poem to that! A twig moved near me and when I bent lower I saw it was an adder. I watched it slide into a clump of grass and disappear. I should have to walk carefully. The thick overhang of trees made it steadily more difficult to see.

When does being alone cease to be enjoyable? Up till now I'd been enjoying my walk, more or less, identifying flora and fauna. But my quest? 'Habitat: tangled hedges. Nest well hidden near ground in brambles and nettles . . .' Merle would be wondering where I had got to.

When does solitude become loneliness? I'm not a nervous chap, and yet, standing there in the dim half-light, the branches laced over my head, nettles stinging my ankles, I felt . . . something. As if, while I listened to the silence, others did the same, deep in the heart of the wood.

And yet, it was an ordinary French wood, the natural result of the ground sloping down on either side, probably a dried-up river bed, nothing sinister, only about a mile from the village, and it wasn't even night. Distantly I heard the clanking of the bells, and that reassured me. The boy was sitting on the hillside because his parents had told him to do so. It was a good thing he'd never known the delight of fruit machines.

And then I heard it clearly, the loud fluid whistle of the oriole, and I felt my heart lift. If I could spot its hiding-place, get myself into a comfortable position, I might be able to photograph it. I had some silly notion that one day, when I retired, I might write a better bird handbook than the one I used.

I slung my camera round on my back, bent down and pushed as silently as I could through the bushes. They were mostly juniper now, and decidedly prickly, but to spur me on I heard the loud 'chuck-chuck-wee-o' clearly ahead of me. About five yards away there was a wall of bushes, all kinds, blocking my path. They tell me you can judge the age of a hedge by the varieties of growth in it, but no matter . . . my eye had just caught, in the confusion of greenery, a glint of gold. This was my lucky day. I dismissed the fact that orioles generally stay on the treetops. I was going to get a fine photograph of it any minute now. I had never learned the art of tracking or camouflage, but somehow by holding my breath and moving very slowly I got up close to the hedge. And there was still the tantalising golden glimmer. I swung my camera round, sighted through the viewfinder and crept forward for the last two or three paces. The thick barrier of bushes was one wall of a small grassy enclosure. I was near enough now to see through the space beyond it.

I dropped my camera against my chest. Two people were lying there. There was a glint of gold all right, but it wasn't an oriole. It was the sun splashing through a gap in the trees on the back of a man's head.

I crept away. 'The male is an unmistakable brilliant yellow.' I walked slowly back to the hotel, hardly noticing the thickets or the flinty path.

Merle was up. 'Any luck?' she asked.

'No, none.' My mind was a jumble of images. Henri, morose, because of his wife. The fair-haired man, the engineer, who we had met. Merle's remark afterwards in the dining room: 'Did you notice the golden glint in his hair?'

'You're quiet, darling,' Merle said.

'Am I? I suppose I'm disappointed. I thought I had spotted a golden oriole, but it wasn't.'

'Never mind. You'll be lucky next time.' I didn't want to tell her about my discovery. Perhaps she would jump to the same conclusion as I had, and somehow I couldn't face that. I cheered up.

'How about a drink before dinner?' I said.

'Good idea. I'm nearly ready.'

When we were sitting at a table outside with our drinks, I held up my glass to the light. It contained an aperitif made of walnuts, principally, another suggestion of Henri's. There was a glint of gold in its depths. 'Glint of gold.' Would that phrase go on repeating itself in my head?

I didn't demur when Merle suggested the following morning that we make tracks for home. It was the children's half term soon, and there were appointments we had to keep.

'Are you still keen to find a cottage here?' I asked her.

'Yes, of course. I admit I was rather put off by that old mill, but I love this place.' We had a chat with Henri and he promised to let us know if anything turned up, and we also spoke to Guy, the joiner, and told him we hoped to employ him if we found a cottage in the village.

It was a glorious morning when we left, and the village looked peaceful and beautiful. Henri and Marie shook hands with us. I searched her face, but didn't see anything there to confirm my suspicions. 'Come back soon,' they both said. We drove away, Merle saying that she had left a little bit of her heart in Bernay, and I agreed. I would put out of my mind my search for the golden oriole, and what I'd seen or thought I'd seen. But I didn't tell Merle. Perhaps I didn't want to spoil her idyll.

Two

When we got home we were plunged into our usual routine. I started to write, with the added incentive that I had to make as much money as I could in order to buy a house in Bernay (we hadn't wavered from our decision), Merle was busy with her voluntary work at a children's home nearby, and then there was our gardening and all the activities in connection with the village.

The children were home for the summer holidays, and we took them up to Scotland for our usual visit to my parents there and our walking and climbing pursuits on the hills. Summer for them meant Scotland; other holidays were for trips abroad with us. Betsy, aged fourteen, and Nick, two years younger, were fond of my parents, and we all cherished our holidays with them in Argyll.

Surprisingly, it was Betsy who was the intrepid climber. Nick was happier with long tramps in the rugged countryside, and he had a particular affinity with my father. They both had quiet, contemplative natures, and I loved seeing them together.

After they went back to school, we settled into the run-up to Christmas. We hadn't any money to go gallivanting; besides, I was busy writing. After Christmas we had a card from Henri and Marie Leroy, with a note written on it that surprised us: 'Marie safely delivered of a son on Christmas Eve. Baby and mother doing well.' Inside there was a scribbled letter from Henri:

Madame Chantal Gibert, the daughter of the owner of the château (remember I told you that he had died three years ago) called to congratulate us. She

17

was telling me that Monsieur Maury, the old man who lives in the cottage between us and the gates of the château, is being taken by his daughter to live in Souillac with her. His cottage will then become vacant, and I mentioned your names to Chantal as possible tenants. She is often there since her divorce. If you are interested, you should write to her at the château. I believe she is spending Christmas there with her children. I do hope you can come to some arrangement with her. It would give me great pleasure to see you established at Bernay.

We were both thrilled, and I wasted no time in writing to Madame Gibert. We also sent a congratulary note to the Leroys with some baby clothes and toys that Merle bought.

A reply came from Madame Gibert after a long time, during which we had quite given up hope of hearing from her. It was now February. She apologized for the delay, saying that she had returned to Paris to settle the children at their schools. Since we were friends of Henri, she said, she would give us first refusal of the cottage when Monsieur Maury left.

We arranged that we would call and see her when next we came to Bernay, probably June.

Life was going well for us in the early part of the year, especially with the prospect of the cottage in Bernay, when the terrible thing happened.

I had come down to the kitchen in my dressing gown one morning, and Merle was at the sink. 'Sorry I'm late,' I said. I had my eyes on her back and she didn't turn. Then, as I looked, I saw her body crumple, and she fell to the floor. No sound, just this awful sight of her lying there, motionless. I was petrified for an instant, then I jumped up and went over to where she lay, kneeling down beside her. My heart seemed to be in my throat, choking me. 'Merle,' I said, 'what's wrong?' She didn't reply, just lay there, her eyes closed, and looking deathly pale. I took one of her hands in mine and rubbed it. I didn't know what to do. 'Merle,' I said. 'Speak to me, please, please . . .' I was shaking, I just knelt there, looking at her, and then I realized I should have to do something. Our neighbours on both sides were elderly, so going to either of them would be a waste of time . . . there was only one thing. I got up, ran to the telephone and dialled 999.

I went back to where she lay, but she hadn't moved. She lay there, looking lifeless. 'Merle,' I whispered, my voice seemed to be stuck in my throat, 'speak to me, please.' What if she never moved? I brushed the thought immediately aside.

It seemed an interminable time before the ambulance arrived. I kept jumping up and going to the window, and at last I saw them stopping at our gate. I opened the door and ran down the drive. I spoke to the men as they were getting out. 'It's my wife! Thank God you've come. She just fell . . . she's unconscious . . .'

One of the men interrupted me. 'Keep calm,' he said. 'Let's get inside.' They unloaded a stretcher and followed me into the house.

I stood in the hall, trembling, listening to the murmuring of their voices. Will they come out and tell me she's dead, I wondered, then found myself praying: 'Please God . . . no, no.' I went and sat on the bottom step of the staircase and put my head in my hands, unable to go into the room.

Then they were there, with Merle on the stretcher, securely strapped in. 'We're taking her to the hospital,' one of them said. 'We think she's had a stroke, or possibly a heart attack. You'd better come along with us.'

I can hardly describe the agony I suffered from then on. I wondered if I should telephone Merle's mother, or the children, then realized that I wouldn't know what to say to them or what was wrong. So I sat for what seemed hours in a side room, where I had been asked to wait by a kindly nurse . . . and waited.

At last, a doctor appeared. 'Mr Woodbridge?' He stood in front of me, a stern-faced man, younger than me, 'Your wife has had a subarachnoid haemorrhage, I'm sorry to say. She's dangerously ill. They happen very suddenly, an aneurysm, basically a bleed to the brain. I can't tell you any more, it's a question of waiting to see developments. Everything to alleviate her condition has been done. We should know the outcome in twenty-four to forty-eight hours. I suggest you go home. We'll get in touch with you if we want you here. Is there anyone who could . . . wait with you?'

'You're not saying she's going to die?' I said. 'I can't take this in . . .' I put my hand to my mouth, which I knew was trembling.

'I know it's terrible for you.' I saw a young man distressed for me, and tried to pull myself together. 'But I'm afraid you'll have to await the outcome.'

'I'll go and tell Merle's mother,' I said

'If you do that,' he said, 'leave telephone numbers with the nurse.'

He led me out and passed me over to the nurse I'd seen before. 'Look after Mr Woodbridge,' he said, then to me, 'We must hope for the best.' He put his hand on my shoulder, then hurried away.

The nurse was kind, saying sympathetic things to cheer me up. 'You're wise to see your wife's mother. She'd like to know, I'm sure. And you need someone. Have you children?' I nodded. 'Tell them too.'

I drove the short distance to Margot's house, dreading the thought of telling her. I'd never felt entirely at ease with her. She was very much the diplomat's widow, and it was she who had insisted on paying for Betsy's and Nick's schooling. I had given in to please Merle.

Her housekeeper opened the door to me. 'Mr Woodbridge! Come in. I'll tell Mrs Strong you're here.'

She left me standing in the hall while she went away, and I thought how different from my parents' home, where my father and mother would be there, welcoming us in, fussing around, and generally looking delighted to see us.

The woman came back, and said, 'Come along, Mr Woodbridge. She'll be pleased to see you. You don't often come at this time.' I didn't reply, and followed her into Margot's drawing room. She was sitting at the oriel window, and she smiled at me, a society smile. 'Well, Martin, what a pleasant surprise! Please sit down.'

I did. 'I have bad news for you, Margot,' I said. 'Merle's in hospital. She's very ill. They thought I should tell you.'

'What's wrong?' Her hand flew to her face. I tried to tell her, but halfway through she stopped me and said, 'We must have her moved to a proper clinic.'

'No,' I said. I bent forward and took her hands. 'Everything is being done that can be done. With something like that, I gather it's touch and go, but we must hope for the best.' Her eyes above her hand were tragic. 'It's a question of waiting . . . She's in good hands, Margot.' I put my hand on her shoulder. 'We'll just have to wait, as they suggest. I'll go home and telephone Betsy and Nick.'

'Yes, do that,' she said. 'No, on second thoughts, phone from here. I'll go and tell Mrs Carter to make us a cup of tea.' She got up. 'There's the telephone beside my chair.' She was weeping now, her handkerchief to her eyes. Merle was her only child. I felt heartily sorry for her.

I phoned the children's schools, and asked to speak to them. I told them their mother was very ill, and that I would phone them again. I felt terrible about doing that, but knew it was the right thing to do. Afterwards I telephoned the hospital, but Merle's condition hadn't altered.

Mrs Carter came in with a tray, followed by Merle's mother. I drank some tea to please her, then she came back with me to the hospital.

We sat through the night in the waiting room, and at periods we were brought more tea. It left an acrid taste in my mouth that I've never forgotten. The nurse was very kind, but I began to lose hope. We didn't speak much, Margot and I. We ran out of words, and I began to hope that someone would come in, even the doctor. I dared not say to Margot that I had a fearful premonition that Merle was going to die. They couldn't face us. That was it, I told myself. The nurse came in again. Her face was solemn. 'Would you like to see her?' she said.

'Has she recovered?' Margot asked, brightening.

'I'm afraid not. You'll have to prepare yourself, Mrs Strong.' She looked at me and said, 'I'm sorry. The doctor thought you'd like to see her . . .' We followed her into the ward. I put my arm round Margot. Merle was lying in a bed behind screens, her body straight under the bedclothes, her face so pale and beautiful that I could hardly bear the pain I felt. I bent over her and kissed her forehead. Margot was weeping. 'Oh, my baby . . .' she said. She was sitting on a chair, and she half fell over the bed, moaning. The nurse was comforting her, but I could do nothing but stand there, feeling the heavy weight of my wife's death in my heart. I'll never get over this, I told myself, then thought of Margot, and the pain she must be feeling. I helped her to her feet, and guided her out of the room.

'What are we going to do, Martin?' she said to me in the car, but I could only shake my head. The youngish doctor had seen us before we left. 'There was nothing we could do,' he said, 'in a case like this, but wait. We had to find out where the aneurysm was. It can bleed in such a way that it gives stroke-like symptoms. Perhaps it was better for your wife this way, considering what the outlook might have been. That may be a small comfort to you. Her death was due to raised intracranial pressure, and unfortunately, there is no recovery from that.' He shook hands with us and left.

Three

I felt a temporary lift in spirits in April when I brought the children home for the Easter holidays. Their company cheered me, and I drove them to Scotland after a day or two spent with Margot. I knew they looked on it as a duty visit. She had aged since Merle's death, and had begun taking holidays abroad with a friend. I could understand this. She probably knew the same restlessness that I suffered from. I had found it more than difficult to write in a house reminding me constantly of Merle, and had begun eating out, on the invitation of friends, but I refused more times than I accepted. The only thing that buoyed me up was the thought of the cottage in Bernay. Madame Gibert had written to me to say Monsieur Maury had now vacated it, and it was mine if I wanted it. It was a difficult decision to make, and I waited until Betsy and Nick were home to decide. They urged me to take it. They were both learning French and said they would love to go to Bernay during holidays. 'And think of boasting to our friends that we have a holiday house in France,' Betsy said. I wasn't sure if I would be able to go back, but realized I had to move forwards. The house had been offered to me. I wrote and accepted.

I made up my mind that I would write diligently until June, finishing off several commissions, and then I'd set out for Bernay. My grief over Merle was best assuaged by writing, and I kept at it. Looking back, I know that was the best work I ever did, at least, judging by the sales of two books, one a novel, another a pseudo-travel book, more about me than travel. I called it *The Inner Eye*, and it took off well.

June came, and I set off in the car, taking 'our' route. I talked to Merle in the car, sang our songs, wept, and arrived

23

at Le Tilleul three days later in time for dinner. Henri welcomed me. I thought he looked older. His energetic air had gone, and there were lines round his eyes. He wasn't like the man who had scaled that stone wall with so little trouble. When I enquired about Marie, he said she was in their cottage, attending to the baby. She didn't spend so much time in the hotel now, he said, and I noticed there was a different woman waiting on the tables. 'But you, Monsieur Woodbridge, my heart grieves for you . . .' I thanked him, unable to say more. Meeting him had brought Merle back to me. I could hear her voice: 'I think I've left a bit of my heart in Bernay.'

'Robert seems to have been promoted,' I said when I had found my voice. 'I saw him going round the room with his notepad, taking orders, quite the maître d'.' Henri nodded, his eyes full of sympathy.

The hotel was full, and I had to share a table with a middle-aged woman, friendly, the type who is used to travelling alone, and when we had exchanged pleasantries, and I had told her I had been here before, she said, 'Ah, but wait, things have changed around here.'

She was right. When Henri banged the coffee machine at the end of the dinner, it had the same effect as the clashing of cymbals. Everyone looked up expectantly. 'Here it comes,' my companion said.

And then, the triumphal entry, split-second timing. Marie, the baby held proudly in her arms, the radiant smile, and her happy voice filling the dining room as she made her way from table to table, 'Bonjour Mesdames, bonjour Messieurs!'

The compliments fell like petals. 'Mais il est ravissant!', 'Comme il est adorable!' Under cover of the blandishments and the baby-talk the woman at my table leant towards me and whispered, 'They were married nine years. No baby. And then last year she got pregnant. He is so proud. He insists on this, I understand.'

'A proud father,' I said. I looked across at Henri. His face was impassive.

'A wanted baby, and a beauty into the bargain. They were

24

lucky,' she said. I wondered if this was a feminine jibe. Henri and Marie were both dark-haired, dark-skinned; I had always thought Marie had beautiful eyes: large, expressive, one might have said, sexy. I noticed, too, that her dark hair now hung down her back, luxurious, midnight black. Previously it had been done up on top of her head. The baby, though, was fair. I mean that his complexion was pink and white, his eyes dark blue, and the sparse hair, growing in a high fringe on his round forehead, held light in it. He had the open, diamond-shaped smile that all the best babies have. '*Le petit roi*,' I murmured. The little king.

And, of course, with the instinct that babies possess, he seemed to be aware of this admiration. When he extended his dimpled hand, I took it. I felt like one of his subjects. When I congratulated Marie, she said, 'Henri likes to show him off.' You could have fooled me, I thought. When I looked towards the bar, I saw Henri leaning on it, following the royal progress with his eyes. He didn't look like a proud father, indeed, he looked . . . gloomy.

I didn't sleep much that night. I thought of Merle, as usual, my longing intensified by being back in Bernay, but as well as that I felt puzzled: there was something worrying me. That baby. Being flaunted. At Henri's command? My dinner companion's words came back to me. 'They were lucky,' she had said. And I had wondered if she meant because the baby was fair.

The next morning I had an appointment with Madame Gibert. She welcomed me at the château with two good-looking children in tow, approximately the same age as Betsy and Nick. She was dark-haired, slim, vivacious and voluble. She gave the impression of someone who had a profession, who could deal with the public, sure of herself. She spoke in little rushes of speech, laughed a lot. Her social self, I thought. Her eyes were intelligent, but they didn't reflect her bright manner; they looked sad. There would be another side to her character, which she was adept at hiding. A compli-cated, modern woman, in contrast to Merle, who had been typically English, quietly-spoken and shy. I used to tease her about her boarding-school manner.

At an early age she had been sent home to a progressive girls' school, but instead of giving her confidence, she told me she had always felt awed by the clever girls there, who thought of and talked about careers. Margot, a domineering woman, imagined Merle would follow in her footsteps and marry early, and had never encouraged her to think otherwise. Her father had always been too engrossed in his work, and only seemed to want Merle to be a copy of her mother, to be a good hostess, and in time a good wife. 'If I had been a boy, he'd have been pleased,' she once said to me. 'He couldn't talk to me because we had nothing in common. I wasn't even in the ladies' cricket team at school.'

Merle and I met when she was eighteen, in her last year at school. I was speaking, along with other supposedly up-and-coming young authors, at a book event in the town. Three of us were invited to an informal meeting at her school, a poet, a novelist, and me, a travel writer. Since I can't remember my companions' names, I don't think that they have become well known. The three of us joked amongst ourselves about the 'crumpet' we would meet, the 'in' word of the time. It was at the bunfight afterwards that I found myself, teacup in hand, speaking to this tall, slim, almost fragile girl, who surprised me with her geographical knowledge. I was hooked, and so, surprisingly, was she, in spite of her shyness. We arranged to meet in London before she flew home, and we had tea together at Claridge's. It wasn't my usual haunt, but I was out to impress. I told her I had fallen in love with her, and she said she felt the same. It was as simple as that.

We had corresponded for a year when she came to London with her mother, who, I think, had been told by her husband to look me over. Apparently, although my profession was not what they liked, my credentials were good, and I was passed. We were married in May of the following year, 1950. She was twenty and I was twenty-four, young enough to be romantic, and believing that one had to get married to enjoy sex with one's affianced.

This woman I was meeting couldn't have been more different than Merle. Marriage hadn't really given Merle more confidence. She never hankered after a career, and once she had reared Betsy and Nick, and we had decided that was the extent of our family because of the difficult time she had had at their births, she occupied herself in helping out at the local children's home. She was naturally good with children, and that and looking after the house and me, seemed to be enough for her. That, I felt would never have satisfied Chantal Gibert.

'How nice to meet you at last, Mr Woodbridge!' She took me in with one all-over glance. 'These are my two children, Mathius and Lenore.' We shook hands. 'We just arrived from Paris last night, a long drive.'

I agreed, but said I liked driving, that distances didn't worry me. 'That was always part of our holiday, my wife and I, when we came to France.' To my embarrassment my voice thickened.

'Ah, yes, you have my condolences, Monsieur. Henri told me you had lost your wife. Much worse than me. I had a marriage of five years and then . . .' She shrugged. 'But my former husband is still alive.' Her children stood to attention beside her. How did they feel, I wondered? I thought of Betsy and Nick, and how we had all stuck together. They had been a great support to me. I hoped I had been the same to them.

'Shall we walk down to the gates and see the cottage?' she said, and I agreed.

It was a pleasant surprise to me, much bigger than I had expected, with three good bedrooms, one on the ground floor and two in the attic. We had agreed on the price by letter and she suggested that we walk back to the château to sign the necessary documents.

'Clinch the deal?' I said smiling.

She repeated the words as we made our way up the wide drive, lined with laurels. 'I love those English expressions,' she laughed.

'I'm very lucky,' I said, 'to be given the chance to buy the cottage. The children are looking forward to it.'

She waved her hand dismissively. 'There were many contenders. It suited me to say that I had already promised it to an English family. Then my father thought a lot of Henri.' She looked at me, an upward glance. 'Have you seen the baby?'

'Yes,' I said, 'a little beauty.' I thought her eyes were twinkling, but then, as I've said, she was vivacious. She led me into a huge room with French windows on to the garden. Her children were there, and she told them to look after me while she got coffee.

'Simone is pretty old now, she had to give up working,' Lenore informed me She was a copy of her mother in looks, dark, and with a maturity that Betsy didn't have, as if she had grown up quicker. I also noticed she was wearing earrings, which Betsy never did. It wasn't the custom then with young girls.

'I'm going to cut the grass for Jean,' Mathius said. 'Mother has put them both in a cottage in the village, but he still tries to come to do the garden.'

'Mathius likes the thought of sitting on that mower,' his sister said to me. I presumed they were referring to some kind of family retainers. And to her brother, 'Bet you can't do it.' They were no different from my two, despite the polite impression they had given when I had been introduced to them. I felt quite at ease with them, and we were laughing together when their mother came back with a laden tray. I noticed Mathius took it from her, and she put her hand on the side of his head, a loving gesture.

'We were comparing schools in England and France,' I said. 'Your two find it amusing that Betsy and Nick still wear uniform.'

'I think that's a good idea,' she nodded. 'Shall they be here for the summer?'

'They're dying to come, to improve their French.' I said.

'*Bon*,' Mathius laughed, 'but perhaps our French will be the kind they won't want to hear.'

Lenore gave her brother an admiring look. His mother said, 'Mathius!' She looked at me, a 'What-would-you-do-with-them' look, and I felt good to be with them.

'Do Betsy and Nick play tennis?' she asked me. She had got their names right.

'Yes,' I said, 'they're both quite keen.'

'We can have some good games,' Lenore said. 'Mathius always beats me.'

I enjoyed my visit to the château, and when I was leaving, I invited them to join me for dinner at the hotel that evening. 'All of us?' Madame Gibert said, laughing.

'Of course.' I liked the children, and it made my invitation easier.

I walked back to the hotel, happier than I'd been since Merle's death. Perhaps it was being with a family again, and being accepted, but as well, the thought of the cottage excited me. The children could spend their holidays there with me, and I could go there any time on my own, or perhaps invite friends. A new kind of life was opening out for me, and it seemed attractive. Chantal Gibert had been very welcoming. I remembered that she didn't know *my* first name. How could I tell her without seeming to presume? I went over in my mind several ways of letting her know: 'My friends call me Martin; "Monsieur" is so formal.' But the thought of an audience of two children put these ideas out of my head. I would have to leave it for the time being.

They arrived at half past seven, smiling, all talking at once. 'Oh, aren't you lucky to stay in a hotel,' Lenore said, 'and have all your meals made for you!' Mathius was lordly in a dark suit, and Lenore appeared to be wearing lipstick. They were allowed to have wine by their mother. She seemed to enjoy her children, appreciate them, in a very un-English way, and even when Mathius, waving his hand to emphasize what he was saying, overturned his glass, she didn't reprimand him, but laughed with Lenore at him. Fortunately we were sitting at a table round the lime tree, so there was no harm done.

'I think we'll have a treat in store when we go in for dinner,' I told them. 'Madame Leroy brings in the baby.'

Mathius looked unimpressed, but Lenore looked at her mother, her eyes shining. 'Lenore adores babies,' her mother said. 'Especially Thibaud. She came with me when we called to extend our congratulations.'

'I suppose you feel the same as me about them, Monsieur

29

Woodbridge,' Mathius said to me, and seizing my opportunity, I said, 'Monsieur makes me feel ancient. My name is Martin.'

'Martin,' his mother repeated, looking at me. 'Nice.'

My dinner companion of the previous night stopped at our table. '*Le petit roi* may not appear tonight. He's having his inoculation this morning. His mother told me.'

I couldn't introduce her as I didn't know her name, but the others heard her. 'What a disappointment,' Lenore said, and her mother put her hand over hers in consolation, her eyes laughing.

But that baby was a real trouper. The show had to go on. True to form, when Henri banged the coffee machine after the meal, he appeared through the swing door in his mother's arms. But this time his mouth was turned down, his big eyes were dark-rimmed, he had a look of suffering that wrung my heart and perhaps was intended to. He extended his little hand to each guest as he was carried round the room. His look said, 'We are grateful for your sympathy,'; the royal 'we'. Lenore was enchanted, Mathius disgusted, and Chantal's eyes were amused when they met mine. 'Just look at Thibaud,' she said.

'*Ah, le pauvre petit!*' '*Quel mechant medecin!*' Murmurs of sympathy were echoing around us. I watched the little mouth turn down even more with all this cluck-clucking, tears come into his great eyes as the sorrowing ladies kissed his little hand.

'What a performance!' Chantal said.

'What a fuss about a baby!' Mathius said, and Chantal and I sat back to listen to the ding-dong battle going on between the two children.

I was sorry that evening when they left me at the cottage to return to the château, but felt somehow I was one of them. After all, I was the owner of the cottage at the château gates. And I had enjoyed Chantal Gibert's company.

After I went home she wrote to me enclosing the documents regarding the sale, and we began a friendly correspondence. I always signed myself 'Martin'. I was glad of it, because of missing Merle, and her attitude was so positive and forward-looking, that she helped me more than she knew. She told me about her work and her children: Mathius, it appeared, was fourteen, Lenore twelve, but there was never any gossip about the village, nor information about herself.

Four

I may say that thanks to the Gibert family, my holiday at Bernay that June was very enjoyable. They were only there for a few days – it was half-term for the children – but during that time, I saw them often in a most informal way. Once when I was working in the garden of the cottage, Chantal Gibert stopped the car at my gate. 'We're going to Souillac to shop,' she said. 'Do you want a lift there?'

I had decided to start on the garden while Pierre, a young man recommended by Guy Rosier, was painting all the inside white. I wanted to erase all signs of Monsieur Maury, who had been addicted to brown. Guy was inside mending windows and putting up shelves for my books. I only hesitated for a minute. I had been thinking of going myself to Souillac to buy furniture, but the men had arrived that morning, and I had put it off. 'They're working inside, so, yes, I'd like to come,' I said, leaning on my spade. 'Could you wait a few minutes while I tidy myself up?' She nodded, smiling. I waved to Lenore and Mathius in the back.

When I came out, she bent forward and opened the passenger seat door for me. 'In here, Martin,' she said, and as I fastened the seat belt, 'You don't mind if I call you that, do you?'

'Not at all.' I said, 'if you don't mind me calling you Chantal.' We laughed at each other.

'Have you anything in mind?' she asked me as we drove towards Souillac.

'If you'll give me some advice, yes,' I said. 'I need some furniture for the cottage, then I can move in.' I had been putting up at the hotel.

'Chantal will give you loads of advice,' Mathius said from the back.

'*Quel toupet*!' she said, laughing. 'I don't expect your two are so naughty.' She glanced at me as she drove. I smiled in reply, thinking of the rapport that seemed to exist between her and her children, quite unlike what our set-up had been. Merle had expected Betsy and Nick to show me respect, because of her own upbringing (her father had been a bit of a martinet). I had tried to strike a different note, but with them away at school for part of the time it was difficult.

'English children are trained at school to be respectful,' Lenore said. I had noticed her habit of laying down the law.

'Some schools,' I said. 'I think it's beginning to change. We had a French girl on an exchange two summers ago, and even at twelve she was much more sophisticated than Betsy.'

'In what way?' came the demand from the back.

'Well, we liked Betsy and Nick to clear off to bed around ten thirty, but Chantal, yes,' I said, turning to look at her mother, 'she was called Chantal, sat at Nick's feet every night after supper, imprisoning him in his chair. He complained about her to me, but, secretly, I think, he liked it. Nothing would shift her.'

'She had fallen in love with him,' said the oracle in the back.

'She had about twenty pairs of earrings with her, and my wife told me she had arranged them all along the window ledge of her room.'

'Well, there's nothing wrong with that,' Lenore said. 'I wouldn't travel without my earrings.'

I felt foolish. 'Oh, we didn't object, how could we, but Betsy didn't even have her ears pierced. She hadn't mentioned it. Chantal was more advanced in her ideas and her conversation than Betsy.' I almost blushed at the remembrance of how we had discussed the poor girl, and the attitudes she had brought into our house. How provincial, I thought now.

'Well, the only jewellery I wear,' Mathius said derisively, 'is my gold chain. And that's on my neck. Girls change earrings to attract men, it's like the preening birds go in for.'

'What nonsense!' Lenore said. 'That's a popular delusion of boys.'

'Well, why do you wear them?'

'There are heaps of reasons, we like changes, and it's lovely to have a collection, and then you can chose one pair to suit what you're wearing, everything has to match, not only in colour but in style . . .'

I listened to the squabbling going on in the back. Merle, who could always be quite strict with our children, would have stopped it long ago. But it let me see what kind of children these in the back were. Mathius, being male, obviously believed he should be dominant; I wondered what their father had been like. I pictured him as dark-haired, dark-suited, arrogant, someone who laid down rules for his family, which wouldn't suit Chantal for long, I thought.

'Would you care to give me some advice as to what I should buy for the cottage?' I said to Chantal. I kept my voice low.

'I'd like that,' she said. She raised her voice. 'You two are in charge of the shopping list for today. I'm going with Martin to help him to buy furniture.'

'I'll take charge of the car keys,' Mathius said.

'All right. Lenore, *cherie*, you take the shopping list and my purse from my handbag. It's in the back. You each may have an ice or a coffee afterwards at Le Divan. We'll meet you there.'

We drove into Souillac across the bridge above the Dordogne. I thought, as Chantal followed the main street, how gracious were the houses on the right-hand side, solid villas, reminding me of a Mediterranean resort. When we reached the Self Service, she turned into the large car park behind it.

We all got out and she locked the car and gave the keys to Mathius and checked with Lenore that she had the written list and the purse. 'Put the shopping in the boot,' she told them, 'but frozen goods must go in the coolbag there. We'll try and not be long. *A toute a l'heure.*'

We set off, Chantal and I crossing at the post office where it looked less busy and descending to the area round the church with its cupolas and statue of Isaiah, the old town a maze of busy little streets. Here one saw the real Souillac, crafts shops that Merle and I had liked to browse round, the patisserie where we had bought such good chocolate éclairs, bread shops, furniture shops where we had often admired the hand-made tables and chairs. I was surprised, therefore, when Chantal led me to a kind of emporium behind the *charcuterie* well known to me for its splendid pâté. 'I know the man who runs this place,' she said. 'He's a real gypsy. Travels around the villages buying up good pieces from the unsuspecting villagers who are throwing it out in favour of the highly polished rubbish on sale today.'

We entered what looked like a huge shed. Seated at a desk at the entrance there was a young man, swarthy, with flashing white teeth. He got up to shake hands with her. 'Well, Madame Gibert,' he said, 'what a pleasant surprise to see you here! What can I do for you?' He had gold rings in his ears, and I saw the flash of gold from a molar when he smiled.

'This is my neighbour in Bernay, Monsieur Woodbridge,' she said. And to me, 'This is my friend Luc Bouvet, he's well known in Souillac for his expertise, *n'est-ce pas*, Luc?' She smiled at him, and he shrugged deprecatingly.

'*Enchanté.*' His handshake was firm. 'You search for something, Monsieur?'

'Indeed I do,' I said. 'I'm furnishing a cottage in Bernay, and I need the usual things.'

'And no reproduction nonsense, Luc,' Chantal said. 'Genuine French provincial. I know you have some hidden away.'

'Very hard to come by, Madame, but if you follow me, I'll see what I can do.'

He did very well for me, thanks to Chantal, who flirted with him shamelessly, I presumed on my behalf. It was certainly effective, because after an hour or so I was the proud possessor of a sturdy table and four chairs for my kitchen, two comfortable sofas for the sitting room, and three beds and chests of drawers for the bedrooms. Various small pieces were selected by Chantal and Monsieur Buvet at knock-down prices. I came away highly satisfied, having made arrangements to have the stuff delivered the following day.

When we joined the children they were comfortably installed at a table with two friends of Mathius's age, to whom I was introduced, The four young adults, I thought, had more *savoir faire* than their English counterparts. 'This table is only for the young, Chantal,' Mathius said laughing, 'you and Martin must find another one.' His friends joined in the laughter.

'Very well,' Chantal said. 'We know when we're not wanted. Come Martin, we'll find another table for *les troisièmes âges*.'

We might be *les troisièmes âges*, retired, yet when I sat down opposite her, for the first time that day I felt awkward. One of Mathius's friends had quipped that probably we wanted to be alone, and I had laughed, not being able to think in French of a suitable reply. The remark remained with me. 'Well,' I said to her, when I had ordered coffee, 'it appears we've been segregated from the young.'

'Does it make you feel old?' she asked, smiling at me provocatively. Her dark eyelashes swept her cheeks, she rested her face on her hands. I thought how good-looking she was in the absolute sense. It was something to do with this place, like the Isaiah, for instance: the proportions were right. The shape of her face was oval, her eyes finely set and pleasing in their dark blue colour, the deep blue of stained glass, and her mouth was finely drawn and, strangely, unrouged. I could see the curved line of her lips etched against the white of the skin round it, the regulation bow shape not requiring any definition by lipstick.

'You seem to be examining me, Martin?' The blue eyes twinkled at me.

'Excuse me,' I said, 'it's a writer's trick. I can't find any flaws.'

'Oh, but there are!' She lifted her fringe, and above her left eye there was the white ridge of a scar, about three inches long.

'How did you get that?' I asked.

'Let's say a skiing accident,' she said. She turned her head away and I guessed she didn't want to talk about it. 'What was your wife like, Martin?' Her eyes were on me again. 'Do you mind me asking?'

36

'Not at all. Well, Merle was a typical English rose. Quite different from you. Shy, but she had definite ideas about how a wife should behave.'

'And how was that?' she asked, her eyes amused.

'It's difficult to explain. Her mother had inculcated ridiculous ideas in her, old-fashioned ideas. That marriage should take up all a woman's time and energy, and that the man was the arbiter in all things, and the children should be taught to be respectful to him. I tried to persuade Merle to take a job, I was very conscious of shutting myself away from her, but she felt she had a role at home. I said I didn't want her to be my slave, but she believed marriage was a career. Just as she believed children needed their mother at home. Then came the rub. She had been sent home to a boarding school in England, and Margot said that her husband had wanted Betsy and Nick to have the same privilege, and money had been set aside for their fees. I agreed, reluctantly, thinking that perhaps it might release Merle to study for a career, but she compromised by offering her services at a local children's home. I'd never come across this colonial outlook before, indeed, I always got the impression from Margot that I wasn't good enough for their daughter. My background was grammar school, an only child, both my parents were civil servants. I don't want you to think Merle was indecisive,' I said, having seen a look of disbelief on Chantal's face. 'She had a will of her own, and could be as stubborn as hell, but this attitude had been dinned into her.'

'Never underestimate the influence of parents. My background was similar to your Merle's, except that we lived in Paris most of the time by necessity, and my mother expected me to marry one of my father's associates. He was an *avocat* – how do you say it? – in the Ministry of Justice.'

'Lawyer, or advocate, I get it. An important position, I should say?'

'I suppose so. There were numerous parties, and as I grew up I was expected to attend. It was at one of these I met my former husband.'

'And now you are divorced?'

'Four years ago. I waited until the children had grown a little.'

'You mean, you wanted to earlier? Forgive me, I shouldn't ask questions.'

'Oh, that's all right. Yes, I knew in a year's time I had made a mistake. I studied law, like my father. I shared another interest with him. He loved Bernay, as I did, it was the family home, and he longed to retire there, which he did when his father died. I'm in a practice in Paris, a women's practice. We deal especially with women's problems. We feel, from the heart,' she put her hand on her own heart, smiling at me, 'that men sometimes give women a hard time of it.' She laughed.

'Perhaps writers are not included in your supposition.'

'I don't think *you* would. Your work has been done on your own, you have never been a member of a pack.'

'So I haven't been tainted?'

'That's about it.' She smiled at me, and I watched how her mouth widened over perfect teeth.

'Your life is so different from Merle's,' I said. 'She would probably have denigrated hers.' And feeling emotional thinking about her, I changed the subject. 'I'm very grateful to you for helping me today.'

'It was fun. Why don't we help you to put things straight?'

This is going too fast, I thought. But then, the children will be there . . . Why was I so affected by this woman? I tried to analyse my feelings, wanting to know her better, mixed with a feeling of betrayal.

'It will also be goodbye for the time being, because we leave for Paris the day after.'

'When shall you be back?'

'August, school holidays. But I'll let you into a secret. I've arranged to have a pool constructed before we come back. I'm keeping it a secret from Lenore and Mathius. I thought it would be nice if they could ask their friends over to swim. You and Betsy and Nick are very welcome to use it too.'

'That's a generous offer.' Tennis, and now swimming . . . but it was typical, I was sure, of her generous nature. I could imagine Merle saying, in similar circumstances, 'Let's keep it to ourselves, Martin.' She had been shy of crowds and always liked to think of us as a closely-knit family, not requiring anyone else. For the first time, I thought how selfish that was. In their own way my parents had always been sharers.

Going back in the car, Chantal said to Mathius and Lenore, 'Martin's furniture is being delivered tomorrow. I thought we could help him to put it in order.'

'I don't mind,' came from Mathius, and Lenore said, more enthusiastically, 'I love arranging things. We have some old stuff in the attics, *Maman*, carpets and things.'

'Please,' I said, 'Don't spoil me. But since you are all so kind, come and have supper with me, then we'll do the arranging, OK?'

There was a chorus of agreement from the back.

Five

In bed that night after Chantal Gibert and her children had gone home, I reviewed the evening. When they arrived, Mathius had been carrying a record player and some records, and Lenore and Chantal bore a large carpet between them. I rushed to help them, protesting when they said it was their house-warming gifts to me.

The whole evening had been hilarious: they had been most enthusiastic, and had set to with a will to turning the little cottage into a home.

The carpet was just right before the sitting-room fire, we arranged the table and four chairs in the kitchen, and while Lenore and Chantal were adding what they called the finishing touches in the bedrooms, Mathius plugged in his record player. Soon an old Cole Porter song from *Kiss me Kate* was wafting to me in the kitchen, where I was preparing a cold supper, a chicken I had bought when we were shopping in Souillac, lots of rounds of chèvre cheese, and, my favourite, a succulent *tarte aux mirabelle* from the baker. As I heard their laughter, I thought of Merle. Would she have approved of this family helping us, had she been here? Somehow I thought not.

When I shouted to them to come and eat, and they had taken their places at the table, I thanked them for their help. 'I couldn't have managed wihout you,' I said. I had poured four glasses of wine and I held mine up. 'Thank you all very much.'

'*N'importe*. We all enjoyed it,' Chantal said. 'Isn't that right?' She waved her glass at Lenore and Mathius, who chorused, '*D'accord!*'

'Anyhow, I'm most grateful,' I said, 'and I shall miss you

when you go back to Paris. You've made my settling-in very easy.'

'When we come back,' Lenore said, 'your children will be here, and we'll be able to have those tennis matches.'

'Yes,' I said, 'they're looking forward to that.' I saw Chantal leaning back in her chair, smiling, and her eyes met mine. 'Here's to the future,' she said. 'No more wine for Lenore and Mathius' – I had lifted the bottle to fill up glasses – 'they've had their ration.' They didn't protest. The singer on the record was now pouring out *'When I fall in love . . .'* and without any embarrassment, Mathius and Chantal joined in, holding out their hands to each other in true duet fashion. She had a husky, attractive voice.

'I thought Juliette Greco had joined us,' I said.

'They do duets together,' Lenore said. 'They're not bad.'

'Thank you.' Mathius and Chantal bowed, and Chantal said, 'Praise indeed,' laughing at her daughter.

We went through the French ritual of kissing when they left, and when I saw them walking away up the drive to the château I felt sad. They had made my arrival very pleasant. And it would have been perfect if Merle had been here. Or would it? Was I experiencing some kind of relief without her? She had never been at ease with people. I could hear her saying, 'This is nice, Martin, just you and me,' after guests had departed. Her attitude had tended to dictate our social life, no big parties, no letting one's hair down. When the children came home from school, she had plans made for the four of us, but they rarely included other people. How would she have liked Chantal? Well, I would never know the answer to that one.

After the Giberts had left for Paris I moved into the hotel again, as I had commissioned Guy to lay a new floor in the sitting room for me. The bedroom ones could be made good, and the kitchen had flags, which I had decided to keep.

It was in between seasons and there were few people staying. The nightly performance with the baby had stopped. I rarely saw Marie, but Henri liked a chat after he had served coffee. We would sit under the lime tree with a last glass of wine. When I asked him how the baby was, he said, 'Fine,' and left it at that. He was certainly not one's picture of a happy father; no proud showing of photographs.

He asked about the cottage, and I told him how kind the Giberts had been to me. 'Chantal's parents, the count and his wife, were also kind to me when I worked there,' he said. 'I had trained as a chef in the Army, and I took over the kitchen when their cook left. They adored Chantal, she was an only child. She liked to come into the kitchen to help me, and she followed me about in the garden. I was by way of being a general factotum. Her marriage was a big affair. Everyone was invited to the château to wish them luck. I can't say I liked her husband, Parisian, very supercilious.But rumours began to circulate that the marriage wasn't a happy one. I don't know how they started, she used to come to the château with the two children, but without her husband, and I certainly thought she looked far from happy. It upset her father. He was very worried about her. Then she began to come home for longer and longer periods, and once or twice Marie, who was a parlour maid there, had seen her crying. I guessed the cause was Monsieur Gibert.'

'He never came back with her?'

'Only at the beginning. He was an advocate, and he got into some legal trouble with his firm. It had to do with money, of course. It was around that time that she came home alone with the children. Someone in the village had read about the case in *Le Monde,* I can't remember the details now, but I'm quite sure Chantal wouldn't have left him if he had been innocent. She was an advocate too, like her father, who had been a judge in Paris before he retired to the château. I believe she worked in the same firm as her husband. Once when I was walking round the gardens with the Count at the château, he confided in me that he had never liked Monsieur Gibert. *He* blamed the death of his wife, who had ailed for a long time, on worry about their daughter's marriage. "But women are so ambitious for their daughters," the count said to me.'

Henri, without looking at me, muttered under his breath, 'We can all make mistakes in marriages.' I wondered if I had heard correctly. He went on, 'Marie never liked Chantal, but I always admired her. She could be headstrong, certainly, but she was always charming to the staff, and we loved her. She was so full of life. Marie said she was autocratic, but that simply wasn't true, and we were always made welcome at the château, even after we moved here, although I had to persuade Marie to go.' He stopped abruptly. 'I'm talking too much. Another glass, Monsieur.' I noticed he didn't pour one for himself.

I said to him that I was sorry I wouldn't be staying at Le Tilleul now, but that I had appreciated his friendship, and hoped the hotel would go on from strength to strength.

'No, Monsieur,' he said. 'I have decided to give it up. I shall wait till after the hunting season so that I can tell my clients.'

'But why?' I asked, surprised. 'You've made a success of it. It seems such a pity. What will you do?'

'I'll leave here,' he said. 'When we bought this place Marie and I were enthusiastic. It was her idea. We worked well together. But since the baby came, she has lost interest in it, and she's needed here. She mopes about the house, and only cares for the baby. There are things about a hotel which can only be done by a woman. I'm busy with the bar and cooking, and we need her to look after the rooms. Curtains and linen have to be replaced, there are countless things like that. We worked as a team but no longer.' There was misery in his face, and in his eyes when they met mine, and I felt I couldn't press him.

'I'm sorry,' I said. 'I wish I could help you. If there is anything . . .'

He shook his head. 'Some sorrows can't be shared. There is one's pride.'

I nodded.

The following day I paid Guy for what he had done, and made arrangements with him to go into the cottage and finish his work. The cost so far was very little, and too, I felt I had made a good friend in him. Indeed, Kent seemed far away, and had it not been for Betsy and Nick I would have willingly stayed on. I could have written here, I knew. Bernay had began to feel like home, and Kent like another world.

I stopped at Henri and Marie's cottage on my way out of

the village. I knocked at the door, and in a minute or two Marie appeared, holding the baby in her arms. He crowed when I took his little hand, and I complimented her on how well he was looking. I couldn't have said the same about her. She had an indoor look, pale, and there were dark shadows under her large brown eyes. There was something wrong, I was sure. 'Another of your suppositions,' Merle would have said.

'I'm leaving today, Marie,' I said. 'I didn't want to go without saying goodbye to you.'

'But you'll be back in Bernay now that you have the cottage. You like it?'

'Very much. When I come back I shall have my children with me.'

'Mathius and Lenore will be companions for them, I'm sure. Lenore,' she shook her head, 'is she still opinionated, like her mother?'

'Most little girls are, I think,' I said, surprised at the comment. 'My Betsy is the same.'

'Chantal ruled the château before she went away to Paris. But she was a changed person when she returned minus a husband.'

I didn't want to discuss Chantal with her, nor indeed marriages. 'Well,' I said, 'I'll say goodbye for the present. And good luck.' I patted the baby's arm.

When I got into the car, I waved to her, and she waved back. She was a pathetic figure, I thought. She had wrecked her own marriage, and was possibly regretting it. The baby in her arms looked so healthy compared with her. His hair had grown since I had last seen him, and his round cheeks were pink and dimpled. She lifted his little arm to make him wave to me. I was glad I hadn't mentioned Henri, nor his intention to give up the hotel.

My mind was full of the Leroys when I drove past the hotel, and although there were a few people sitting at the tables round the lime tree, there was no sign of Henri. I remembered Merle and me driving into the square when the sun was setting, both of us feeling we had found what we were looking for. Now I had found a house here, and it would probably play a large part in our lives, the children and myself, but no Merle. My eyes filled, and as I drove towards Souillac, the fields on either side of the road were blurred. I saw the woman with her goats, as though through a veil, but as my eyes cleared and I gathered speed, I realized there was a car a long way in front of me. Without intending to, I drew close to it. There was only one occupant, the driver, a fair-haired man. As I watched he turned down the road to the old mill where we had been with Henri. I knew who the man was. Had he come at Henri's request, to see the water tower, or to see Marie again? I was leaving a mystery behind me, and if it was solved while I was away, I would certainly hear when I got back.

I was in Limoges before I had shaken myself free of memories of Bernay, the hotel, Henri and Marie, and the baby, and Chantal Gibert and her children. There were plenty of reasons why I should go back. I had promised Chantal to keep an eye on the swimming pool that was being installed, and I wanted to know what had happened with the Leroys. And this time I hadn't been to the *causse* down the tunnelled path. Was it because of the memories that were associated with it? The flowers Merle had loved so much, or the memory of my discovery of the two people making love? I didn't speculate on the outcome.

When I got back to our house in Kent, I phoned the schools and spoke to Betsy and Nick and made arrangements when to pick them up. I telephoned Margot's house, but her housekeeper told me she was still away. It was a rainy, miserable night, and I made myself some supper and went to bed. My spirits were volatile. I lay sleepless most of the night.

The English weather seemed to compound my feeling of not belonging in our village. It was deserted when I went to shop the following morning for essentials, but I should have remembered it was a commuter village, and Merle had usually done the shopping while I worked. I knew I wouldn't miss it when I went back to Bernay; indeed Merle and I had only chosen it for its proximity to the coast and France. And now I was going back without her. 'Trying to catch up on the news?' the man in the village shop asked me when I bought a paper. I had told him I'd been in France. He lifted his head from the cash register when he was getting me my change. 'I was sorry to hear you had lost your wife,' he said. I got the impression that he was implying that I shouldn't have gone on holiday since Merle had died, then realized I was feeling paranoid and I'd better be friendly.

'Thank you,' I said. 'But I have a house in France, so I shall be away quite a lot.' He gave me one of those some-folks-have-all-the-luck kind of looks, and said, 'That's five pounds and three pence, thank you.'

I thanked him and left the shop.

In the afternoon I decided to work in the garden. The house seemed so empty and depressing. I was now grieving deeply for Merle. Everywhere I looked I saw signs of her, in the kitchen, in our bedroom. I had cleared out most of her things after her death, but it was her presence. It was there. The garden seemed an escape, and I was busy cutting the lawn when I saw a man opening the gate and coming towards me. I saw as he came nearer he was wearing a dog collar, so I arranged my face to welcome him.

'Hello!' he said, as he came up to me. 'Busy I see. I'm Donald Macintosh, your friendly vicar.' He had red hair, blue eyes, and a strong chin. He looked as Scottish as his name.

'It's kind of you to look in,' I said. I took a quick glance at my watch. 'Time for a drink. Will you join me?'

'Delighted.' He followed me into the house. When I had settled him in an armchair with his preferred tipple, Scotch and water, we talked for a long time. I told him about Betsy and Nick, and he told me of his three children, Hazel, Megan and James. We both agreed that they were a blessing, and he said, 'Why not come to us for dinner tomorrow and meet the family? Our house is not like yours,' he added. 'I see the signs of a good housewife here, but ours is the kind of place where you fall over things if you're not careful. Then we have two dogs and a cat.'

'It sounds good to me,' I said. 'I'd be pleased to come.' After that I would only have two days to go before the weekend, when I would pick up the children. My mood had changed. Thanks to this man, life seemed possible again.

'I spoke to your wife when she came to church,' Donald Macintosh said. 'Such a gentle, pretty woman. I was at a diocesan meeting on the day of the funeral, so my curate had to officiate. I was sorry about that. That's really the reason for my visit, to apologize.' He got up to go.

'No need to apologize,' I said, when I was showing him out. 'I'm glad to meet you. And I'll look forward to meeting your family tomorrow evening.'

'Seven o'clock? We like the family to eat with us. There's a great virtue in all getting together round the table. I'm sure the children will remember it when they go out into the world.' I thought, it's remarks like that which make me dislike the clergy, then mentally chastised myself for being cynical. Merle would have agreed with him. Village life in France suited me better. One felt one could be as peculiar as one liked, and the villagers would be less judgemental. The French left you alone to be yourself. I know some would not agree with me.

When he had gone I went upstairs to my study and went on with the book I was working on. When Merle and I had stayed in Loches I had become interested in Agnès Sorel, who had lived there in the fifteenth century. She had been renowned for her beauty, and had become the mistress of Charles the Seventh of France. We had seen her burial place in the collegiate church of St Ours, and on the way home we had stopped at the Tours library to allow me to read up on her. I had even written a book on her, though my agent had yet to sell it to a publisher. Those holidays in France . . . My heart filled, and possibly my eyes.

Agnès Sorel had been a sweet woman, unlike the usual courtesan. I remembered her carved face in the church. Like Merle's.

I set off the next evening to have dinner at the vicar's house. I was greeted by a red-haired woman, who said she was Jean Macintosh, and that Donald would be home shortly. He had been called out to the bedside of an old man who was dying. She left me in their sitting room with the children, all red-haired, not surprisingly considering their parents, and I immediately got on their right side by telling them about Betsy and Nick. Hazel, the eldest, about Nick's age, said that, 'Mummy had asked their Mummy to bring them round for Saturday tea, but she had said that they didn't go out to tea, that you all went walking on Saturday afternoon. Mummy thought it rather rude since she had asked them.'

The three of them looked accusingly at me, and I thought, they're not as easy to get on with as Lenore and Mathius.

My correspondence with Chantal helped me through this time in Kent. I had the feeling that I was waiting to get back to Bernay, so great a hold it had on me. The letters I exchanged with Chantal were a great comfort. She told me about her life in Paris, and I told her about England. I wrote to tell her about my visit to the vicarage, and saying that this was typical; she replied saying that she thought it was sweet, and very much like Bernay.

I went with a feeling of great relief to pick up the children from school. I was pleased to see that they both looked well. Betsy made our supper and Nick lit the fire. They cheered up the place for me, and we agreed to set off at the weekend for France. As usual we enjoyed the crossing, and the meal on the ferry, and we put up at a good hotel. They chattered all the time, and made the journey enjoyable for me. Betsy was very interested in anything I could tell her about the Giberts, but Nick was quieter as I drove rapidly through France. He said to me as we were passing through Uzerche, 'This is the first time we haven't had Mummy with us.' He was sitting beside me, but Betsy heard him from the back and said, 'Nick, you promised not to upset Daddy!'

I said he hadn't upset me at all, and we must talk about Mummy whenever we felt like it, resulting in an outburst of anecdotes from Betsy: 'Do you remember when Mummy bought me a china basket from that shop in Limoges?' and such like.

'Now you're doing it,' Nick said.

When we arrived at Bernay they were charmed with the village, and also the cottage. Guy Rosier had finished the floor of the sitting room, and he, or his wife, had put a blue vase of zinnias on the table. They ran about the cottage, choosing their rooms, Betsy deciding on the one that had a small door into the loft, because she loved mysterious little doors in rooms, and Nick pleased with his choice because he could see the château from it. I went to bed, feeling happy with our new house.

Six

The next morning after we had tidied up I took the children down the tunnelled path behind the church. Betsy was excited about the wild flowers, but I persuaded her to wait till we came back to pick them. We were going to the *causse*, and when we got there, they were both captivated by its expanse and the marvellous views. We sat there for a long time, and just as if it had been yesterday, the boy who was taking care of his flock, passed us by. *'Bonjour,'* he said, his eyes on the children. He must be the same age as Nick, I thought, but shouldn't he be at school? A mystery; perhaps we could ask him some time.

As we were walking back, I cast my eyes at the path I'd taken when I'd been in search of the golden oriole. On our way to the *causse* I hadn't allowed myself to look.

'There's another path,' Nick said, pointing. 'I wonder where it goes.'

'I took it once,' I said, 'looking for a golden oriole. They're supposed to frequent here, or hereabouts.'

'Were you lucky?' he asked.

I shook my head. 'No, let's push on. Betsy's disappeared.'

'She's picking flowers', he said. 'I expect you came here often with Mummy?'

'Yes, you know her passion for flowers. She loved it here.'

'I like the *causse* but not this path, particularly.' He looked at me apologetically. 'But then I'm not into flowers.'

'We'll do some birdwatching together,' I said to him, 'and when the Giberts come, you'll have tennis and swimming. We'll take a stroll through the grounds of the château this afternoon and see how the pool's getting on.' I had told Betsy and Nick about it, and they'd been excited at the thought.

'What if they don't like us?' Betsy had said, and I had assured her that they were great fun, and they were looking forward to meeting her and Nick.

We were walking through the village en route for Le Tilleul – I had said I'd give them lunch there – when we met Monsier Vincennes, the priest. We shook hands, and I introduced him to Betsy and Nick.

'We're on our way to have lunch at Le Tilleul,' I said. His face showed immediate concern. He glanced at the children, then put his hand on my shoulder and guided me away a few steps. He spoke quietly.

'You haven't heard? Henri has been taken into custody. A man's body was discovered in the old mill,' he whispered. 'Marie has been questioned also. It's a terrible thing for the village. We are all under suspicion.'

I was shocked. 'Terrible,' I said. I immediately thought of having seen the fair-haired man turning into the road to the mill, when I was leaving Bernay. 'So the hotel is closed?'

'Yes, Marie is with her mother in Souillac, and the baby. Everyone seems to be staying indoors. Have you noticed how quiet it is?'

'Yes, I suppose so.' I had a thought. 'Will Madame Gibert know?'

'I don't know. I believe she is in Paris.' He looked across at Betsy and Nick. 'Your children are getting restless. If you want to have a talk with me, call this afternoon. I'm always in.'

He walked back with me to where the children stood. 'Excuse us,' he said. 'A village matter. And how do you like your house in Bernay?'

'It's very nice,' Nick said.

'We love it,' Betsy added. 'We've been having a walk around with Daddy.'

'Splendid! And when the Gibert children come, you will have companions.'

He shook hands with the three of us when we left him, and I said to the children, 'There's been a tragedy, and the hotel is shut meantime. Let's drive to Souillac and eat there.'

When I passed the road leading to the mill, I looked down

it, but didn't see any signs of life. But I had seen the fair-haired man driving down there when I was behind him on my way home to England. There was no doubt about it. I should have to go to the *Gendarmerie* and tell them what I knew.

Souillac was bustling with traffic and people, and we had difficuly finding an empty table in the café I had gone to with Chantal. 'I like it here,' Betsy said. 'Shops and things.' I had thought since Merle died that I would have to find someone who could help Betsy in ways I couldn't, feminine ways. Margot hadn't offered.

'Bernay is miles better,' Nick said. 'Dad and I are going to do some birdwatching.'

'I'm going to do some housework and arrange my flowers. Mummy would like to think we were keeping the cottage nice.' Nick nodded.

We all had *Croques Monsieurs*, and while we were eating I told them about the tragedy at the mill. 'It's hard for me to believe,' I said. 'I was friendly with Henri and Marie, and there's a baby. Monsieur Vincennes, the priest, told me that everyone was being questioned. Since I was here fairly recently, and the man was found recently, I feel I should go to the police headquarters and give them an account of my movements.'

'They'll know about you, Dad,' Nick said. 'They're bound to call to see you.'

'You're right,' I said, 'but since I'm here, I might as well save them the trouble. You two can have a walk round the old town, and see the church. Go into the Tourist Office and ask for some brochures. Try out your French, eh? I'll meet you back here, in, say, a couple of hours.'

I gave them some money with instructions to buy anything they fancied for supper, and left them. As I crossed the road to go to the post office to look up the directory for the address of the *Gendarmerie*, I couldn't believe what had happened. I remembered my talk with Henri before I left, and hoped I would be able to recollect the details when and if the police questioned me.

I felt selfishly sorry that this incident had taken place when

52

I had just brought the children. The fact that Henri had been taken into custody must mean that he was a suspect. Murder? I must try not to let it affect the children's holiday here. My decision to go to the *Gendarmerie* might take a long time. Should I go? I decided I would present myself at least, and leave it to them.

In the event my decision had been wise. When I told the *gendarme* on duty that I had a house in Bernay and that I had been there recently, he told me that the detective on that case was out at present. 'If you care to give me your address, I could ask him to call and see you.' We arranged an appointment at the cottage for tomorrow at ten o'clock, and I left, convinced that I had done the right thing.

On my way back to the café I passed a jewellery shop, and on an impulse, went inside and asked to see some earrings suitable for a young girl. The young woman said she thought she had just what I wanted, and showed me a pair that she said were just what I was looking for. '*Regardez*,' she said. 'Little enamelled flowers, marguerites, set in silver. So delicate.'

I liked them, and thought so might Betsy, and said I would take them. She parcelled them the way most shop assistants do in France, expertly, in pretty paper with a rosette of ribbon.

I was quite proud of myself as I left the shop. But Nick? I couldn't leave him out. I went into a nearby Maison de la Presse, the French equivalent of a W.H. Smith, and found a birdwatching book, well illustrated, which I bought. I looked up golden oriole to make sure it was featured.

I met the children at the café. They were there, looking, I thought, a little forlorn. I felt a wave of tenderness towards them, and realized that they had only me. I had been grieving for Merle, forgetting how they must be suffering too. 'I wasn't so long as I thought,' I said. 'The policeman will call and see me tomorrow morning.'

'That's what I said,' Nick nodded sagely, and Betsy said, 'I wonder what a French policeman looks like.'

'Well, you'll know tomorrow.' I put my presents on the table. 'The one with the ribbons is for Betsy, in case you didn't guess.'

Their faces lit up. 'Thank you, Daddy,' Betsy said, leaning forward to kiss me.

'Open them now if you like,' I said, 'and if they don't suit, we can take them back.' While they were busy I ordered three coffees.

Betsy seemed delighted with the earrings. 'They're beautiful, Daddy. They must have cost you a bomb.'

'No, just half a bomb.'

'You have to have your ears pierced for these.' Nick was the expert. 'This is absolutely right, Dad,' he said, waving the book. 'Thanks. I've looked up golden oriole, and it's in here.'

'Good,' I said. 'And don't worry about the ear piercing, Betsy. We'll ask Madame Gibert where you can have it done. Indeed, she might go with you.'

'That would be great!'

We drove back to Bernay, and when I passed the hotel, it looked deserted. What would Merle have thought, if she'd been here? She would have been upset, I knew.

I decided not to call and see the priest, and after we had had some tea and patisseries, which Betsy had bought, we set off for the château. A middle-aged woman opened the door to us. 'I'm Madame Vilar from the village. I keep an eye on things for Madame Gibert.'

'She asked me to look in and see how the pool was getting on. I live in Monsieur Maury's cottage and these are my children, Betsy and Nick.'

She shook hands with us, and told me to go ahead. 'The men have just left off,' she said.

We walked down the drive again, and we were just turning in to the place where the pool was being installed, when a car came up the drive. The driver braked, and I saw it was Chantal Gibert. She leaned out and said, 'Hello Martin! These are your children?'

'Yes, Betsy and Nick. We were just going to see how the pool was getting on.'

'How good of you. I don't have my children with me,' she said to Betsy and Nick. 'They're still at school.' And then to me: 'I offered to return when the *Gendarmerie* telephoned me about the Leroys.'

I nodded. 'I've just been to Souillac. Someone is coming to interview me tomorrow. Perhaps he'll make arrangements to call and see you at the same time.'

'It's dreadful, poor Henri. I could scarcely believe it when I was told.' She stopped short, looking at the children. 'I'll get out and we'll go and see the pool together.' When she did, she shook hands with Betsy and Nick, kissing Betsy. 'You've got the same mixture as I have,' she said, laughing at me. 'Lenore and Mathius are looking forward to meeting you two.' The children were smiling, looking pleased.

The pool was well ahead, with the tiling half done, and a start had been made on the flagging round it. 'It's getting on,' I said. 'Another week should see it finished, don't you think?'

'There's the filling of it,' Chantal said. 'I don't know how long that takes.'

'You've chosen a good place for it,' Nick said. 'I have a friend at school, and they had to cut down several trees to get the sun.'

Chantal said, 'You're smart to notice that, Nick. This piece of garden used to be my father's rose bed. Actually they never grew very well, and as it was flat, and gets loads of sun, I thought it was just right. Then it's sheltered from the wind by the bulk of the château.'

I was pleased with Nick, and listened with some pride to the conversation between Chantal and him.

'Why don't you come down to us for dinner?' I said to her. 'Betsy and I can manage that between us.' I was so happy at seeing Chantal that I surprised myself with my invitation.

Chantal smiled at Betsy. 'I'm sure you're a good cook, Betsy. Yes, I'd love that. What time?' she appealed to me.

'Eight o'clock?'

'I'll be there.' This time she went through the ritual of kissing the three of us on either cheek before she got into her car.

'Well, what do you think of her?' I said to the children as I walked back with them to our cottage.

'She knows a lot about pools,' Nick said.

'She's stunning,' Betsy said. 'I loved her leather jacket.'

Her look was so wistful that I registered that a leather jacket would be a suitable present for next Christmas.

The cottage was looking cosy when Chantal arrived. Nick had lit a fire in the sitting room and Betsy had arranged her flowers. She and I had got busy in the kitchen while Nick set the table. Chantal had discarded the leather jacket and was now wearing a white dress and earrings, which I saw Betsy eyeing.

'How lovely this is,' Chantal said. 'I'm quite envious.'

We sat in the sitting room and chatted, and I poured out some Sauvignon Blanc for us. I thought I would follow her example, and asked Betsy and Nick if they would like some. They both nodded, looking pleased, but, unlike Chantal, I was careful to underfill their glasses. I had also put bottles of sparkling water on the table in the kitchen. Merle had never allowed them to have any alcohol. I left Chantal chatting to Betsy and Nick while I went into the kitchen to see if everything was in order. Betsy had been to the delicatessen and bought a supply of sliced meat, pâtés and so on, and we had plenty of ice cream in the freezer, as well as some patisserie and a bowl of fruit. Betsy had laid out the cold meats on a large plate, and I had made a salad with basil from the garden and olive oil to make the leaves and tomatoes tastier.

Everything seemed all right. I went back to the sitting room. Betsy was listening entranced to Chantal, who was evidently telling her about pierced ears. Nick sent me a masculine glance.

'Dinner is served,' I said.

Chantal got up. 'Betsy and I are having an interesting conversation about earrings,' she said.

'I was admiring Madame Gibert's,' Betsy said. 'They're diamonds.'

'Ah,' I said. 'Well, this is beyond Nick and me.'

'I shall take Betsy to Souillac to have her ears pierced, if you permit it,' Chantal said. 'She has shown me the ones you bought for her today. They are adorable.'

'I expect you're a connoisseuse,' I said. 'I'm sure Betsy would be delighted to go to Souillac with you.'

56

'Dad bought me a birdwatcher book,' Nick said. 'There's a golden oriole in it.'

'Ah, yes,' Chantal said, 'they are indigenous here.' She looked at me. Chantal Gibert had a gift with children, there was no doubt. She could come down to their level and bring them up to hers with equal ease. I watched Betsy and Nick warming to her, and when they went up to bed, they didn't seem to object to being kissed on both cheeks.

'They're a credit to you and your wife,' she said, when we were sitting at the fire with a last glass of wine. 'And now, what about this tragedy about the Leroys? You were right not to bring it up this evening. It might colour the children's opinion about Bernay. First impressions, you know.'

'It's dreadful! I can scarcely believe it. The reason I went to the *Gendarmerie* this afternoon was that, after you had gone to Paris, I left for home a few days later. I was driving along the road to Souillac when I saw a fair-haired man in a car in front of me. He turned down the road to the mill. I took him to be the engineer who came to see to the water supply at the hotel. It was when I arrived back here with the children that we met Monsieur Vincennes, and he told me that Henri had been taken into custody. Do you really think he's a suspect?'

'Well, if he hasn't confessed, they will be able to test his gun for fingerprints, if they can find it.'

'Shot? Monsieur Vincennes didn't tell me that.'

'I was told on the telephone.'

'So the scenario as we see it is that Henri perhaps had an altercation with Marie and accused her of having had an affair with . . .?'

'Raymond Baron, he's called.'

'Is he? Do you think Marie would tell Henri where he was? Perhaps it had been his hideout and their meeting place, or Henri had heard rumours, and he stole down there at night and shot him? Do you think the police found the gun?'

'So many questions, Martin. No, he would dispose of it. Possibly in the river.'

'Right.'

'The baby, Thibaud, is at the root of this case, obviously.'

'Merle and I found this Raymond Baron a bit of an enigma when we met him at the hotel.'

'A seducer? People talk in villages. I had heard from Madame Vilar, who caretakes for me with her husband when I have to be in Paris, that there were rumours going about. That Henri had guessed the baby wasn't his, and there were numerous quarrels between him and Marie.'

'A *crime passionel*? I've heard that in France this is looked upon more leniently by courts.'

'That depends,' Chantal said. 'You and I are fortunate in a way, Martin. My marriage broke up because my husband was charged with stealing money from the firm. But having powerful relations in the court saved him.'

'And my marriage has been broken by losing Merle.'

She leant forward and put her hand over mine, in sympathy. 'This episode with the Leroys prevents us from feeling sorry for ourselves. I have taken care that it doesn't affect my children. I shouldn't like yours to be affected by what has happened here.'

'Nor should I. But we must take care and not discuss it before them. Unfortunately someone is coming from headquarters tomorrow morning to take a statement from me. I volunteered some information to them this afternoon.'

'What did you say?'

'That I had seen Raymond Baron driving down the mill road. Also that I knew the Leroys very well.' Chantal's eyes were fixed on me. I remembered she was an *avocat*. 'I thought it best.'

'Yes, you were right, my dear Englishman, but don't worry, I too volunteered to come home so that they could ask me anything they wish. I hope to go back tomorrow some time. My reason was my desire to help them in their enquiries. I know Henri and Marie very well. I shall answer any questions they like to put to me.'

'But, of course, you know the ropes.'

She smiled at me. '"Know the ropes". That's one for Mathius' notebook. Now, I must be going, or we'll be causing another scandal in the village.'

'I'm glad you're here. I'll hope to see you tomorrow

before you go away. We'll get together and you can tell me if I've comported myself well with the *gendarmes*.'

We were at the outside door, and instead of kissing me on either cheek, she put her hands on my shoulders and brushed my mouth with hers. 'Dear Martin,' she said, 'you'll do all right. You have an honest face.'

I laughed, and wanted to put my arms round her, but she had slipped away through the open door. I thought of her in bed that night, and what I had kept back. After all, there was no need for me to mention it. It would only make me look like a peeping Tom. That's another one for Chantal and Mathius's notebook, I thought.

Seven

The next morning we were all very jolly at breakfast. Both children exclaimed at the views from their windows, and Nick was intent on getting a bird feeder or making one. 'Madame Gibert is very smart,' Betsy said, 'I hope she will take me to Souillac to have my ears pierced.' I assured her that if she said it, she would, but that she was a very busy lady. And I said to Nick that I would take him to Guy later and ask him if he could make him a bird feeder, or show him how to do it himself. They went off to buy some bread while I waited for the detective to call.

He came promptly at ten o'clock in a black Peugeot, which I thought was sensible. A police car stopping at my door could have aroused interest in the village. He was a man about my age, bespectacled, with a wry smile, and we got settled down in the kitchen. I made coffee for us, and he started right away. He had introduced himself as Detective Inspector Pierre Galimard.

'I knew you were in residence here, Monsieur Woodbridge,' he said, 'but it was good of you to look in yesterday at Souillac. Now, I want you to tell me what you know about Monsieur and Madame Leroy. Any detail might help us in our enquiry, even if you think it is of no account.'

I began. 'My wife and I came to Bernay for the first time in May 1966. We stayed in Le Tilleul. There weren't many guests at that time and we formed a friendship with the Leroys. My wife died in February of this year.'

'My condolences, Monsieur,' he said. 'Will this be painful for you?'

'Looking backwards always is, but if it's necessary, I'm pleased to help in any way I can.' I, of course, kept a diary, as most writers do, and I had looked it up last night in bed, even making notes. It had brought memories of Merle back to me.

'It's helpful to me to be able to build a rounded picture of the Leroys,' Detective Inspector Galimard was saying. 'It is like a crossword puzzle, you understand, and everyone in this village has something to offer.'

'I understand that,' I said. 'Well, as I said, we liked the Leroys very much. The first night we stayed at the hotel we met a fair-haired man, an engineer, who had come to inspect the water tower. Henri was having trouble with the water supply. We entered into conversation with this man when we were having a pre-dinner drink. We didn't like him particularly. Well, you know how it is, you begin talking. His remarks weren't in the best of taste, we thought.'

'Can you give me an example?' Galimard asked.

I thought. 'There was one remark he made that jarred somewhat with us. He had told us he was a birdwatcher, and I said I was interested in spotting the golden oriole. When I asked him if he had been lucky, he said, "In more ways than one."' I looked at the detective. He flicked his head backwards in a nod of agreement, and made a gesture for me to go on. 'Another thing I remember, this man—' The Detective Inspector interrupted me.

'He's called Raymond Baron.'

I nodded. Chantal had told me. 'Mr Baron said that Marie had told him Henri had been asked to carry up water for a guest's bath, an Englishwoman. He appeared to find this amusing. Merle and I both noticed this.'

'In bad taste?'

'I thought so.'

'You said you were friendly with Monsieur Leroy. How did this manifest itself?'

I thought for a moment. 'Well, he took us fishing by the old mill. He was sitting outside his cottage one afternoon when I passed. I've consulted my diary and that would be on Monday afternoon, the ninth of May. I remembered Marie had talked to me about his liking for fishing. Anyhow, I brought that into our conversation. It appeared to cheer him up, and he suggested we go the next day.'

'He took you to the old mill on the river?'

'Yes. Myself and my wife. While Henri and I were talking Merle looked around the mill. She found signs of someone having slept in one of the rooms – she had looked through a broken window – and she came back to tell us. I remember how pale she looked. We thought it could have been a tramp.'

'Did Monsieur Leroy seem disturbed?'

'No. I don't remember him having been affected.'

'Did he seem quite familiar with his surroundings?'

'Very. He said it was his favourite spot for fishing. He seemed to like it. He had a dog with him, Papillon, and he told us that it wouldn't go past the mill.'

'Was he upset about that?'

'No, he didn't appear to be. I thought that perhaps the dog was sensitive to atmosphere, as my wife was.'

'Interesting,' the detective said. 'Go on, please, Monsieur Woodbridge.'

'That's about it. We didn't go fishing again, indeed Henri didn't offer to take us, and the next day when I saw him sitting in the same place he seemed very morose. I had a talk with the priest whom I met afterwards, and he said Henri was the only one who would go down to the mill.' I suddenly remembered. 'I think there was a simple explanation. The miller's daughter had been drowned there.'

He nodded. 'That could be the reason. So you saw Monsieur Leroy sitting outside his house on two occasions? What time of the day was this?'

'After lunch. I presumed he was taking a break. He said his wife was resting in bed, and that she didn't like to be disturbed. I got the impression that she had given him strict instructions to that effect.' I hesitated. Here was the crunch. I supposed what I could say now to Galimard was circumstantial evidence, and yet I hesitated.

'There is something else?' the detective said.

'I don't know if it's of any importance.'

'Suppose you let me be the judge of that.'

'I didn't even tell my wife this.' Nor Chantal, I thought. 'On the Wednesday, the day after our fishing trip, Henri was once again sitting outside his cottage, and he seemed very morose. He didn't make another date for fishing. I spoke for a few minutes, and decided to go for a walk alone. My wife was resting. This, of course, was last year. Do you want to hear this?'

'Please. It's background.'

'I went on down the path behind the church leading to the *causse*. I had taken my camera with the intention of going birdwatching where the path runs into a dip halfway to the *causse*. I had noticed a track there before, intersecting the main one, and had thought it was a likely place to find a golden oriole. I went along this track, being very quiet, and finding it difficult because of the growth of bushes and so on. Then I thought I saw a glimpse of gold through the trees. I thought it must be the golden oriole. I crept towards it and came upon a grassy enclosure. The gold I had seen was the sun shining on the back of a man's head, a fair-haired man. There were were two people there, a man and a woman.' My story seemed ridiculous as I told it. 'Perhaps I had jumped to a conclusion . . .' I looked at Galimard.

'No, you know what you saw, and if you hadn't told me, you would have worried about keeping it to yourself. I know you're an intelligent man and you can work out dates as well as I can.' He gave me a piercing look. 'I'm glad you told me that. May 1966, eh?'

'Yes. I have my old diary at home. I could give you dates . . .' He waved his hand.

'That's all right.' We exchanged looks. Is he calculating as I calculated, I wondered? The baby, Thibaud, there when I came next June, born at Christmas. Henri had sent me a card.

I broke the silence. 'Despite everything, Merle and I were so taken by Bernay that I had asked Henri to look out for a house for us. As it happened this cottage was vacated by an old man after we left, and Henri, on my behalf, spoke to the owner of it, Madame Gibert at the château.'

'I know her.'

I nodded. I wouldn't say anything about Chantal that might be misinterpreted.

'So you were offered the cottage?'

'In due course. It was a difficult decision to make. My wife had died. I have two children, and they liked the idea, so when Madame Gibert offered it to me, I took it.'

'Quite. We haven't talked about the Leroy baby. Had you known about it before you arrived in June this year?'

'Yes, we had a Christmas card from Henri telling us of its safe arrival, the Christmas after our first stay at Bernay.'

His look was quizzical. 'When did you first see it, I should have said "him"? I believe he's called Thibaud.'

'Yes. In June this year, I had arranged to meet Madame Gibert to fix up about the cottage. I stayed in Le Tilleul afterwards. Of course, I saw Henri, but Marie was no longer helping him. He complained to me about this, and indeed mentioned that he thought he would sell the hotel after the hunting season. He had told me of the men who came every year to hunt wild boar, and I gathered that he liked to join them.'

'He would have a gun, then.'

'I presume so. I'm not a shooting man, except with a camera.' The detective smiled.

'Did you see any difference in Henri and Marie Leroy on this visit?'

'Yes, Henri was not the same cheerful fellow I had known, and as I told you, Marie wasn't taking any part in the running of the hotel.'

'And the baby, Thibaud?'

'I saw him when I went to say goodbye to her when I was going back to England. I had to return to pick up my children from school and bring them here. Oh, and I saw him when Marie walked round the dining-room tables in the evening with him. I may be wrong but I got the impression that it was a kind of command performance. Henri didn't look happy.'

'Bizarre.' He smiled. 'You must be weary, Monsieur Woodbridge, and I apologize for troubling you. But what you have told me has been very helpful. This man, Monsieur Baron, did you come across him any other time? In the village, for instance.'

'Never at the hotel nor in the village. But when I was driving away from Bernay towards Souillac, after my visit to buy the cottage, I saw a fair-haired man in a car in front of me. It turned down the road to the mill.'

'Interesting.' He leaned forward. 'When was that?'

'Let me see. This is July the thirteenth. I arrived yesterday with the children, and on my previous visit to buy the cottage, I left Bernay to go back to England on the . . . fortunately, I keep a diary . . . I have it here, June twenty-eighth.' I took it out and consulted it. 'Yes, that's right.'

He looked pleased. 'Thank you, Monsieur Woodbridge. You've been most helpful. Very lucid. But I believe you're a writer?' I nodded. But not of thrillers, I wanted to say. 'I'll leave you in peace now, and I hope we won't have to bother you again.'

'If I've been of any help . . .' As I said that, I realized that what I had told this man might be another nail, or several nails, in Henri's coffin, which was sad. I would be glad to see Chantal when she had been interviewed, to compare notes.

I saw her car stopping at the front of the house when we were having a late lunch. 'Madame Gibert,' I said, rising. 'She'll be on her way to Paris. Go on eating, kids.'

I got up quickly and went into the hall to open the door to her.

She was wearing a black suit and a white blouse, her hair was pulled back from her face. She looked trim and lovely, I thought. 'I haven't much time,' she said. 'I've got to get to Paris tonight. I have an important case tomorrow morning, but I wondered how you had got on with Galimard,'

'Come in for a few minutes at least,' I said, 'and I'll tell you.'

'All right.'

I led her into the sitting room. 'You've had your lunch?' I asked her.

'All I want. I liked Galimard. Very astute. Did you?'

'Yes, I got on very well. He kept his cards very close to his chest.' I saw her eyes light up at the English expression. 'That's another one,' I said. 'I told him that I had seen Baron driving down the road to the mill, and that I had thought he might be camping there.'

'Yes, you told me that. And you think that somehow Henri knew he was there, and went down and shot him?'

'Don't you?'

'Remember I know Marie and Henri very well.'

'Yes, of course. Were you able to help Galimard?'

'I think so.'

'Of course, you're an *avocat.*'

She shrugged. 'I also have a very good intuition where women are concerned. Look, Martin, it will be a fortnight before I'm back with the children. If anything develops I'll ring or write.'

'Thanks.' She looked very much the businesswoman, smart and slender, I thought. Very different from Merle.

Eight

We fell into an easy routine after Chantal had left. I got up about six in the morning and wrote for two hours. I liked to reread what I had written the day before and get going on the next part, leaving it ready to start again in the evening. I would then have a shower and prepare breakfast for the children, who usually began stirring about eight o'clock. After tidying up we set off for Souillac some time in the morning to shop for lunch and anything else we might need. I liked to buy an English paper and have a coffee in our favourite pavement café; I think Betsy and Nick liked to watch the traffic. I didn't miss England. Sometimes as a treat we had lunch in a restaurant with a pool in the old town. We kept swimming gear in the car for this contingency.

In the afternoon I often had a look in at the château to have a chat with the Vilars and see how the men were getting on with the pool. Occasionally Betsy and Nick had a game of tennis together; Monsieur Vilar said that he had permission to open the court for them, if they wished. We would have a walk, taking notes as we went for a map of the village and its environs which we were drawing at the cottage, and often we went to see Guy Rosier. He had said he would supervise Nick in making a bird feeder, and Nick was taking this very seriously indeed, also making nesting boxes for the trees in our garden. He carried his birdwatching book with him wherever we went, and Betsy picked flowers for a book where she kept them, duly pressed and labelled.

I noticed that the Vilars didn't discuss Henri and Marie, but Guy told us that the whole village was shocked. Henri was a great favourite, and they had all been delighted when he opened the hotel. 'It was partly Marie's idea,' Guy told me. 'She pushed Henri on. She had a great influence on him. She came from Souillac, so she had city ways. I wouldn't have called Souillac a city, but I suppose it depended on where you were looking from. On the whole I was impressed by the lack of rumour going round the village. Everyone seemed on Henri's side, or at least, stood by him, a village lad. Marie had been liked too, but there were the rumours that went round about . . . well, one knew that Souillac girls were different.'

A week after Chantal had left, the pool was finished, and there was a little party of the workmen, the Vilars, Betsy, Nick and me, to watch the turning-on of the water. It was a lovely sight. The blueness of the pool echoed the blueness of the sky and from the drive the sight of the château with the pool in front of it was very pleasant indeed. Steps led down from the large flagged terrace in front of the château to the pool, bordered by rose bushes transported from the beds that the pool had displaced. I took pictures of it when it was filled, and Betsy, Nick and I added a stone dolphin from a sculptor's yard we discovered in Souillac to stand at one end of it. Everyone was thrilled, although Madame Vilar shook her head and wondered what the old count would have thought of it.

That night when I was working upstairs, I phoned Chantal. I heard her voice, bright, '*Allô, Chantal Gibert.*'

'This is Martin Woodbridge, Chantal,' I said. 'How are you?'

'Tired. I've been in the courts all day. But how nice to hear from you!'

'I'm phoning to report,' I said. 'You will be pleased to know that the pool is finished and filled. It looks lovely!'

'*Admirable!*' she said. 'The children will be pleased. They finish school tomorrow, and we shall be in Bernay in a few days. If you and your children wish to swim in it, please do so.'

'I wouldn't dream of it,' I said. 'It's yours. You must be the first.'

'The English are so correct. In that case, I shall have a party for its opening once we arrive at Bernay. You, Betsy and Nick will be amongst my guests.'

'That sounds good!' I couldn't think of anything to say. 'Are you well?' I asked.

'Yes, thank you. But I have not your luck, to be a writer and choose your time to work.'

'That's true. But I will never manage to persuade non-writers that it's hard work.'

'You can try when I return.' There was a teasing quality to her voice that Merle's had never had. But why did I compare the two women? It was obvious that comparisons were odious. Chantal's life had been quite different from Merle's, who had always implied by her attitudes that she had to be taken care of. Anyone who lived with Chantal might find it quite the opposite. 'Martin?'

'Yes, I'm here. The children have quite taken to the lifestyle here and are looking forward to meeting your two.'

'You don't mention the Leroys.'

'No. There is nothing I can tell you. I haven't heard any gossip about them, nor have I heard from Detective Inspector Galimard.'

'I'm keeping my eyes and ears open here. I'll let you know if I hear any gossip amongst my colleagues. I've seen reports of the affair in the press.'

'It's strange how the papers pick up gossip. I grieve for the two of them.'

'I too.' There was a pause. Neither of us seemed to have anything more to say. 'I'll say goodbye now.'

'Goodbye,' I said. And then, on impulse, 'I'll look forward to seeing you again.' The aura of her personality remained with me and prevented me from concentrating on my work. I went downstairs and found Betsy and Nick watching a cartoon on television.

'Improving your French?' I teased them.

'They're good,' Nick said. 'Remember when we bought these books of Asterix, and the customs asked you to open your case?'

'Yes, I do. And how amused he was. "You like our little man?" he asked me. Anyhow, he didn't confiscate them. They're still at home. By the way,' I said, 'I rang Madame Gibert to tell her that the pool was finished. She's going to have an opening party when she comes to the château next week with her children.'

'I wonder if they'll be stuck up,' Betsy said.

'Don't be silly,' Nick said. 'Honestly, you girls . . .'

'Well, we're like the poor relations here, using all their facilities.'

'Facilities!' Nick laughed. 'Listen to her, Dad.'

Betsy's comments struck home with me. She was right in a way. Perhaps it did put me in an uncomfortable position, accepting favours from the lady of the château. 'She's a generous woman,' I said feebly.

'Well, anyhow,' Betsy said. 'I hope she can spare the time to take me to have my ears pierced before the party.'

'If she doesn't, I shall,' I said.

'No,' she said, 'that wouldn't do.'

'I can't see you swanning into wherever they do it with Betsy,' Nick said.

Betsy's remarks about Chantal Gibert came back to me when I was in bed that night. Anyone married to her might have to play second fiddle to her and her busy lifestyle. It hadn't been like that with Merle. Had it been a marriage of equals, I found myself wondering now? And wondering what it would be like to be married to someone as self-assured as Chantal. Good God! I chided myself. What are you thinking of? Nevertheless, in that delightful time between sleep and wakefulness, my mind wandered along paths that surprised me.

I hadn't given much thought to my relationship to Merle. I suppose she flattered my ego. From there my mind drifted to the Leroys. 'There is one's pride,' Henri had said. Marie had spurned him in favour of another man. Naturally his pride in himself had been severely damaged, and he would want justice. But, I thought, half asleep, supposing the fair-haired man had spurned Marie? Wouldn't she want justice too?

Nine

We were out when the Giberts returned. We had gone further afield that day and visited Rocamadour. I had told the children about the Templars, those bearded white knights in the thirteenth century. 'They had *commanderies* dotted all over the *causse,* and they might have visited Rocamadour which was on the pilgrimage route for St. James at Compostela, ' I had said. The Knights Templars' history had always intrigued me ever since I had taught at Figeac, where I had access to books on the subject. Although Nick had a glimmering of knowledge about them, Betsy was totally in ignorance. When we arrived at Rocamadour, they were, of course, impressed by its situation. Who wouldn't be, with that towering cliff face?

And Betsy was thrilled when we saw a pilgrim wearing a black cloak, the hat with a cockle shell in front and with a staff in his hand. Both children were immediately fired with the desire to walk the route themselves. 'So you should when you're older,' I agreed, but suggested that we should meantime climb the pilgrim's steps to the *Chapelle Miraculeuse* to see the Infant Jesus and the Black Virgin. I joked about it being a steep climb for me, and that I'd have to copy the pilgrims who had gone up on their hands and knees. Of course the children teased me while they went up the stone steps like antelopes. The atmosphere in the dimly-lit chapel was powerful, and one could begin to understand its appeal in the thirteenth century. It quietened us, anyhow.

'I'll take you to the Souillac library soon,' I promised them on the way home.

In the kitchen we were still talking about the Knights Templar and Rocamadour when there was a knock on the door. I laid down the knife I was cutting tomatoes with. 'Who can that be?' I said. I walked through the hall and opened the door. Chantal Gibert was standing there. 'Hello!' she said. 'I thought I'd let you know that we're established at the château. We arrived last night.' I felt instant pleasure at seeing her. Gone was the business outfit. She was wearing a strapped dress, and her hair was loose, falling to her shoulders. 'Would the three of you come to dinner this evening?'

'We'd love that! Won't you come in?'

'No, thanks. Are you all right?'

'Yes. How about you?'

'Glad to be back home.'

'Come in and have a drink.'

'No, thank you. I have a meal to prepare. Tonight, then, seven o'clock? Oh, and if it's fine, we'll be swimming in the afternoon. You're very welcome to join us.'

'Thank you. I'll tell the children.'

'Goodbye.'

'Goodbye.' I watched her going down the path before I shut the door.

When I went back to the kitchen, two pairs of eyes raised to mine. 'That was Madame Gibert,' I said. 'We're invited for dinner tonight, and a swim in the afternoon, if it's fine.'

'Are her children with her?' Betsy asked.

'Oh, yes.' I seized the kitchen knife and went on with cutting the tomatoes.

'Why didn't she phone?' Nick asked me. I shrugged.

'Maybe it's more polite in France to call,' Betsy said.

I had thought the atmosphere in the church at Rocamadour had been, well, powerful. It was nothing compared to that in our kitchen. Or was I imagining it? Anyhow the discussion about the Knights Templar had been knocked on the head.

'I hope it stays fine for swimming,' I said.

'It's misty,' Betsy said, straight-faced.

Nick went on with washing lettuce at the sink. Talk about being sent to Coventry! I thought.

We set off in the afternoon, around four o'clock. The car was stuffed with all our swimming gear. The mist had gone, and the sun was hot and glorious. When we arrived at the château there seemed to be quite a few people seated round the pool. Chantal rose from her seat. She was wearing a black bathing suit, with a colourful towelling jacket and a white bandeau on her hair. What the hell was happening to me? I had never been in the habit of noticing women's clothes.

'Here you are! Now, everyone, you must meet our English friends! First of all,' she smiled at me, 'this is Monsieur Martin Woodbridge, and these are his children, Betsy and Nick.' There was a great deal of handshaking. Chantal went on round her guests. 'This is my friend and neighbour, Ana Lavare and her twin sons, Benoît and Jean. They live nearby and have come to compare our pool with theirs. Isn't that so, Ana?'

The woman, fair-haired, blue-eyed and wearing a blue swimsuit, waved her hand and said, '*Pas du tout*. Ours is old, as you know, Chantal. I only inspired you.'

Chantal waved hers in dismissal. 'And the Woodbridge children haven't met mine. Here they are.' She had an arm round each of their shoulders. 'Lenore and Mathius. Mathius is the older.' He bowed. Lenore said, 'We've heard a lot about you from *Maman*.'

Betsy said, 'We've heard a lot about you too.'

'And we mustn't forget Benoît and Jean,' Chantal said, pushing them forward. 'The irrepressible twins.' They were very alike, tall, slim and black-haired, and they bowed in unison.

'Well, supposing you children get into the pool while we talk about you,' Chantal said. 'Martin, come and sit with Ana and me. Here!' she patted a chair between them.

'Thanks,' I said, and sat down. Ana Lavare turned to me immediately. 'I was sorry to hear from Chantal that your wife died just after you had been here with her, last year.'

'Yes,' I said. 'It was a bitter blow. She had liked Bernay so much.'

'Well, at least you and your children will be able to enjoy it, now that you have a house here. It becomes quite a lively place from now on. The Parisian mob will soon be arriving.'

'Have they all got houses here?'

'Oh, yes, perhaps you haven't noticed how many are shut up, and those who haven't a house stay at the hotel.'

Her glance was meaningful. She wants me to comment about the Leroys, I thought. Chantal, who evidently had been listening, in between directing the children, said, 'Henri is in custody, you know, Ana. We all think it better not to discuss it.'

'I have no intention of doing that, Chantal.' She turned to me. 'It's a pity, all the same, that you arrived when Bernay was under a cloud, so to speak.'

'It doesn't affect me,' I said. I looked at the children playing in the pool. 'They're all enjoying themselves,' I said.

'Do you swim, Mr Woodbridge?'

'Not as well as your sons.' I had been watching them. They were doing a fast crawl up and down the pool, and the others had cleared to the sides to give them room. Hogging it, I thought. Ana Lavare got up and walked to the pool. I could see she was speaking to her sons, but I couldn't hear what she was saying. She came back and sat down again. 'There is such a thing as good manners. One has to be strict, don't you find, Chantal?'

'In my case yes. But you have Maurice to lay down the law.'

'But he isn't always at home. Paris has a lot to offer.'

'Personally I like to clear out and come down here. I always take my holiday to suit the schools.'

'Maurice isn't prepared to do that. As you know he likes to leave time for his skiing. And so do I.'

I got the impression, listening to this conversation, that there wasn't too much love lost between Ana Lavare and Chantal. After a time I gathered up the children and promised to be back for dinner at seven o'clock.

'Seven for eight now,' Chantal said. 'Ana and the twins are coming back, and Maurice, her husband.'

'Maurice will be driving back from Paris tonight,' Ana Lavare said to me.

'I shall look forward to meeting him,' I said. Male support was useful.

I sat in the kitchen while the children were pegging out

their swimming gear. When they came back I had iced orange juice drinks ready.

'Well, then. What did you think of the Gibert children?' I asked them.

'I must say I liked Mathius,' Nick said. 'Sensible chap. Bit older than me. But I didn't think much of the Lavare twins.'

'I liked Benoît,' Betsy said. 'Quite dashing.'

'Are you sure you don't mean Jean?'

'No, I don't. Benoît has smaller ears than his brother. He says that's how people always distinguish them.'

'So small ears are in?' I said.

'So are white bandeaux,' my daughter said. I ignored that.

I sat in the garden with my drink while they were having showers and getting ready for going out. It was difficult being left with two children who were as observant as mine. Strange I hadn't noticed it before. It seemed they had grown up since Merle had died. Or had she kept us all together in her own way? My job was to make friends with them, and if that meant some occasional quips, so be it. Chantal had been part of a one-parent family since her divorce, and she seemed to have an easy relationship with her children. I should have to try and copy her. Betsy came into the garden wearing a fresh red outfit, and headed towards me where I was sitting in a small paved area at the foot of it. 'How do you like it?' She whirled in front of me.

'The colour suits you. The scarlet lady,' I said.

'I get tired of the inevitable blue,' she said in a grown-up fashion.

'Yes, I can quite understand that,' I said, straight-faced. 'It's a pity you hadn't your ears pierced. But those pearls of Mummy's look well on you.' I thought how pretty she looked, and hoped the small-eared Benoît didn't think so too. I decided I didn't trust him. It was a new feeling for me to have. A desire to protect my daughter from any marauding males.

Nick was easy. He had on light trousers and shirt, and looked how he should, a schoolboy with clean nails and hair sleeked back, and an easy smile. 'Time you got dressed for the ball, Dad,' he said. 'We're ready. I thought Betsy was never going to come out of that bathroom!'

He was right to hurry me. I spent some precious minutes choosing a tie after I had showered. I didn't have a dinner jacket with me, and decided I would buy a white linen one the next time we went to Souillac. And I'd take Betsy to have her ears pierced. I was beginning to realize how much it meant to her. We wouldn't wait for Chantal to offer.

Chantal had had chairs placed round the pool and the Lavares were already there. The twins looked immaculate. I studied Benoît's ears, and yes, they were smaller than his brother's, and the man who got up to be introduced to us was an older edition of the twins, except that he had a thin line of moustache along his lip. I couldn't decide about his ears.

'Have you driven from Paris this evening?' I asked him, having been introduced.

'I have.' His smile slipped along under the moustache. 'I find it restful after a busy day.'

'And we only have half a mile to walk and we arrive after you!' I said.

'Perhaps you have never known pressure, Mr Woodbridge. I understand you're a writer.'

'I am. But most writers would agree with me. The pressure to finish a book to suit a publisher is quite something.'

'I must accept that.' He raised his voice. 'Boys! Don't hang around. Take a walk round the garden. Lenore and Mathius can be the leaders. I daresay the Woodbridges would like to join you. Don't you agree, Chantal? Or am I doing what Ana accuses me of doing, controlling?'

'You are being yourself, Maurice,' his wife said.

He threw back his head and laughed. 'Now you know the reputation I have with the ladies, Mr Woodbridge,' he said to me. I had been watching the children trailing off. Interestingly enough, Mathius had disregarded Maurice Lavare's suggestion and placed himself at the top of the line with Nick, and they were chatting happily to each other. Neither Benoît nor Jean were paying any attention to Betsy, and had fallen in behind the two boys. She and Lenore had joined ranks and seemed to have a lot to say to each other at the back of the little procession.

'They'll be happier having a walk round the garden than having to listen to adult conversation,' I said. 'I can remember hiding under the table in my parents' dining room to keep out of the way.'

Maurice Lavare let out another hearty laugh. It didn't take much, I thought. 'And no doubt you picked up some interesting remarks,' he said. 'And saw some pretty legs.'

'No doubt. If I had, I certainly don't remember.'

Chantal walked up to the château beside me when the children had returned. Betsy had seen an owl and was excited about it, even more so than she had been about Benoît. 'Lenore tells me the babies are entrancing with little owl faces,' she said. She reminded me of Merle in her enthusiasm.

'You'll have to come back in spring for that,' Chantal said. 'Possibly Easter. But you must come late one evening and creep into the barn with Lenore and bring a torch. You'll be able to watch the parent birds flying about.' She went on with what she had been saying to me, in response to a polite remark of mine about how she coped with running the château. 'I prepare the meal. Cooking is one of my pleasures. Madame Vilar keeps an eye on things, and her husband waits on table. I'm hoping I may be able to persuade them to move in to the château permanently.'

The dining room was impressive with its tall windows and red-shaded lamps all around. They lit up the old furniture and made the glass sparkle. There was a beautiful centrepiece of roses on the table.

'Chantal has so many attributes,' Maurice Lavare said to me as she seated us. 'Flower arranging is only one of them, n'est-ce pas, Chantal?'

'And I have no attributes,' Ana Lavare said. 'I hate cooking. Perhaps that is why Maurice doesn't hurry home.'

'The secret is in growing your own produce,' Chantal said. 'But I am lucky. Monsieur Vilar is superb in both the flower and vegetable garden.'

'There you are, Ana,' Maurice Lavare said. 'We must find a Monsieur Vilar.'

'Perhaps if you didn't spend as much time in Paris, Maurice, you would have the time to find one.'

'I'd love to work in the garden, *Maman*,' Jean said.

'But your father wants you to be at the Lycee in Paris studying.'

'Poor Jean,' Chantal said. 'Torn in two directions, whether to be a Paris gentleman or a country gentleman. But it's up to you in the end. Mathius has already made up his mind, haven't you?'

'Yes. I intend to study law in Paris, make a lot of money and then become a country gentleman.'

Maurice Lavare roared with laughter.

'*Comme il est intelligent!*' Ana Lavare said. 'And how about your children, Mr Woodbridge? Have you influenced them at all?'

'I'd like to be a writer, like Daddy,' Betsy said. 'But Nick says the same. So I don't know how that will work out.'

Chantal clapped her hands. 'Just think of it. All competing with each other! You are going to have to . . . how do you say it, "look to your laurels", Martin?'

'How charming this conversation is!' Maurice Lavare said. 'In Paris it becomes dull, the latest gossip and the market.'

'Perhaps, then, you should come to Bernay more often,' Chantal said. 'I love family parties.'

'That's what I often tell him,' Ana Lavare nodded.

Is this Bernay conversation, I thought, with everyone scoring points off each other!? I wanted to say. I thought I saw a look of relief on Betsy's and Nick's faces when Chantal said, 'There are drinks on the terrace for all you young people. We are going into the drawing room for coffee.'

I wondered what the conversation was going to be like when we sat down there.

'Now, Chantal,' Maurice said, 'are we going to be permitted to discuss the scandal?'

'You mean Marie and Henri Leroy. Remember, I know them very well, they both worked here.'

'That makes your opinion more valuable.'

'My profession has taught me reticence.'

'Oh, you're incorrigible!' He turned to me. 'Well, Martin,

if I may call you that after such a short acquaintance, were you surprised at hearing of it?'

'Surprised, yes. One always imagines such things happen anywhere but where you are.'

'Do you think Henri is guilty?' Ana Lavare asked me.

'It's difficult to believe it of him. He was such an affable fellow. But there are circumstances . . .'

'Such as Marie having a lover? That doesn't surprise me. She had very come-hither eyes,' Maurice Lavare said.

'Well, well,' his wife said. 'Come-hither eyes! You would certainly be able to recognize such eyes.'

'Oh, come, Ana,' Chantal was laughing. 'Poor Maurice!'

'I don't require you to defend me, Chantal,' Maurice Lavare said. 'Thank you very much.' They were all laughing and I joined in to be sociable. The conversation here was just as barbed as it had been in the dining room.

After a reasonable time I rose to my feet, feeling like a prig. 'I think I must collect the children and go home now.' And adding for Maurice Lavare's benefit, 'I have some writing I must finish tonight.'

'Have we offended you, Mr Woodbridge?' Ana Lavare said.

I looked at Chantal. Her face was quite serious. 'Must you go?'

I had to stick to my guns. We had arrived late, so we should leave early. That sounded like Merle, I thought. 'I'm afraid so.' I smiled at her. 'You must remember, I'm new to being the sole parent to my two, and I feel Merle would have told me not to let them be up too late.'

I saw Maurice Lavare looking at me. I thought it was a look of barely-concealed merriment which he would vent at my expense when I had gone. But I'm a stubborn chap. 'I'll say goodbye, Monsieur and Madame Lavare.' I held out my hand. 'I hope we meet again.'

Chantal accompanied me down the steps to where the children were larking round the pool. 'Sorry, kids,' I said to Betsy and Nick. 'I'm breaking up the party.'

'We're ready,' Betsy said. And to Chantal, 'Thank you very much for having us. We've had a super time, the swimming and food, and oh, everything!' I saw hints of Merle in her demeanour.

'Yes,' Nick said, shaking hands. 'Thanks very much. It was super.'

They both stood beside me, calling goodbye to the rest of the children then walking with me to the car. 'I haven't forgotten about the ear-piercing, Betsy,' Chantal said. She had walked with us. 'How would tomorrow morning suit you?'

'That would be great! Thanks. What time?'

'Ten thirty?'

'OK.'

Chantal stood waving to us as I drove away, and I waited for a complaint from the children.

Betsy said, 'I'm glad you came for us, Daddy. I was getting tired of it. And trying to speak French all the time is wearisome.'

'I liked the Gibert kids,' Nick said, 'especially Mathius. I think we could be good friends, if I'm not too young for him.'

'But not the twins?' I said.

'No, they're show-offs.'

'I think I've gone off Benoît,' Betsy said.

'Despite his ears?' I ventured. I waited for her riposte.

'Yes. I agree with Nick. They're both show-offs. Like their father.'

I kept my mouth shut. Merle had always considered it bad form to discuss guests, or people we had been visiting.

Ten

Promptly at ten thirty, Chantal arrived, with Lenore in tow. I brought them into the kitchen where we were tidying up. 'I see you have Betsy and Nick well organized,' Chantal said.

'We help Josephine too,' Lenore said.

'Who's Josephine?' Betsy asked.

'Madame Vilar,' Chantal said. 'I find that easier to say than Josephine.'

'Perhaps her husband has a different name for her?' I said.

'What would you suggest?'

'Jo,' I said.

'Josie,' said Nick.

'Somehow those don't fit our Madame Vilar,' Chantal said, laughing. 'I could take the easy way out and call her "Vilar", as my father might have done, but I know Madame Vilar. She's always been a very dignified lady. Unlike Simone, who couldn't have been dignified if she'd tried.'

'I like Simone, she brought us up,' Lenore said.

'I must take you to see Simone and her husband sometime,' Chantal said. 'A dear couple who brought us all up. They live in the village.'

'Mathius and Lenore have told me about them, To change the subject,' I said. 'Would you allow me to drive you Lenore and Betsy to Souillac? I have some shopping to do for myself.'

'Daddy's getting quite clothes-conscious,' Betsy said. 'He wants a white jacket for evening wear.'

'You don't have to tell everyone, Betsy,' I said.

'Now you've embarrassed him.' Nick laughed at me.

Perhaps Chantal realized my discomfiture. Instead of joining in the laughter, she said, 'Nick. Mathius is going

81

birdwatching this morning. If you want to join him and you don't want to come to Souillac, why don't you go up to the château? He's waiting for you.'

'Is he?' Nick's face lit up.

'Take my camera,' I said, 'and see if you can get some shots of the golden oriole.'

'May I? Oh, thanks, Dad.' He went out of the kitchen like a bolt of lightning.

'Well, that's two happy birdwatchers,' Chantal said. 'Yes, we'll accept your offer, Martin.'

She sat beside me at the front and Betsy and Lenore chattered happily at the back. I noticed Betsy's French seemed quite adequate as far as Lenore was concerned. On the other hand, Lenore seemed willing to finish every hesitant sentence for her.

Chantal had a great gift for small talk. I didn't have to say much as she chattered away until she said, 'You haven't heard from Detective Galimard?'

'No,' I said. 'Have you any idea when the trial will take place?'

'It will take some time,' she said, 'but he promised to come and see me. I thought I might ask him to the pool-warming party. He lives in Cahors, and I happen to know he has a young wife. I could ask both of them. It might give him the opportunity to speak to me.'

'Good idea,' I said. 'Have you chosen a date for your party? I ask because the children were asking me last night when we were going home. Not that they want to, but just, they know me, I usually want to be back in England to see my agent after a few weeks.'

'Yes, I understand. I'm in the same position. I have several cases coming up in September.'

'You have a very busy life, Chantal. Should you hate to give it up?'

'Why do you ask?'

'Curiosity, I expect. Merle didn't work except for some voluntary duty at a nearby home for tubercular children, so I'm curious, I suppose.' Why are you asking this, I thought.

'I'll tell you the truth,' she said. 'I have to work to keep this place going and my flat in Paris. But I'd willingly give up my work. I enjoy it, it fills my life, but . . .'

'But what?'

'There are other things in life than work. And one doesn't get any younger.'

'What age are you?' I kept my voice low.

She whispered, 'Thirty-five.'

'I'm forty.' And I added, 'Just right.'

'What are you two whispering about?' Lenore said.

'Secrets,' Chantal said. 'Grown-ups are allowed to have secrets too.'

The two at the back tittered with laughter.

Chantal and I looked at each other, and for the first time I saw something in her eyes concerning me. Something that included me.

We parked in the car park behind the supermarket and I parted from Chantal and the two girls, making my way to the old town, where I remembered seeing a men's shop near the cathedral. When I found it and looked in the window, I wondered if it weren't too young for me: the owner evidently had an eye for colour and had his windows dressed with summer clothes for men, colourful shirts, jackets and good-looking espadrilles that I coveted. I went in and was greeted by a young man, smartly suited.

'I'm looking for a white jacket for evening wear,' I told him.

'I think I could fit you,' he said. 'Have a seat.'

He disappeared for some time and returned with several jackets over his arm. 'If you would care to try these on,' he said, 'it will give me some idea of your size.'

I tried them all on, to please him. They all had a different cut from what I was used to, and when I pointed this out to him, he said, 'The Italian cut seems to be popular with the young. But you're the blazer type.' He eyed me. 'I have a blue one here, but you particularly want white. Anyhow, try it on for size.'

I felt at home in the jacket. 'A nice fit,' I said, admiring myself in the mirror.

'Perfect with white trousers.' He seemed to look askance at my jeans.

'Yes,' I said, recognizing a sales pitch, 'but it has to be white.'

'*D'accord*. But I'll be surprised if I've got this in white.' He looked doubtful. 'However, let's hope for the best. I have a large stockroom behind, and if you don't mind waiting I'll search through it. The classic white doesn't shift so well as the coloured with the young. It's colour they're after. My wife will bring you a coffee.'

'Thank you,' I said, wondering if this would mean I'd have to take the blue one.

In a few minutes, a dark-haired young woman appeared carrying a tray with a cup of coffee on it, a small silver jug and sugar bowl. She smiled at me. 'I'm sure Marcel will find what you want,' she said, 'he's very proud of his stock, and tries to suit everyone. Sugar?' I shook my head. 'Cream?' I shook my head again. I accepted the coffee with thanks. She was very pretty, and reminded me of Chantal in her colouring.

When I had nearly finished my coffee, her husband returned bearing a white jacket triumphantly. 'Success!' he said, waving it.

'Your wife said you would find it,' I said.

'Ah, Yvonne believes in me. So necessary in a marriage!'

Of course it was a perfect fit, and after duly admiring myself in the glass, taking particular note of the shoulders, as pointed out by Marcel, I also bought a pair of black trousers which he said must be worn with such a fine jacket for evening wear. I left the shop, bearing my parcel, and was waved off the premises by Marcel and Yvonne. I wondered if he used her as a decoy, because when she was called from the back premises to see me clad in the white jacket and black trousers, she had put her hands together under her chin and said, '*Parfait!*', and rolled her eyes as if she had been quite overcome.

When I met Chantal with the two girls, we all had mutual causes for celebration. Betsy had gold rings in her ears, they were called 'sleepers', I was told, and the three of them were wearing flimsy scarves of voile in fetching colours, which Chantal had bought. I declared my purchases had been quite to my satisfaction, and since we were all pleased with ourselves, I suggested we should go to the hotel across from the supermarket and have lunch. It was four o'clock when we got back to Bernay after a most successful day.

Chantal said she would have to get back and write invitations for her party, which she would make for a fortnight hence. She asked to see my calendar in the kitchen, and said, 'Yes,' counting, 'twenty-sixth of August? Does that fit in with your plans to return to England?' and I said it did, but not to consider me in choosing her date.

'Oh, Daddy,' Betsy said, 'you know we are all looking forward to it, and wasn't that why you bought a white jacket?'

Chantal's eyes were twinkling as she looked at me, and she said, 'Poor Martin!'

I said, laughing, 'Would you send that son of mine back right away if he has returned from birdwatching?' and she was smiling when she said she would.

When she and Lenore had left Betsy said, 'Don't you want to go to the pool-warming party?'

'Of course I do,' I said, 'but if it goes on like this we'll soon be living in the château.'

'There's nothing wrong with that,' she said as she left me, feeling ousted.

Nick returned from the château, highly excited. 'You'll never guess, Dad. I think I've got a picture of the golden oriole.'

'No!' I said. 'Where?'

'In that track which bisects the path to the *causse*. Mathius and I were walking along it, keeping our eyes skinned, when suddenly there it was right in front of us, on the path. We stopped walking and speaking and I snapped it. It flew away, and for a long time we stalked it. It seemed to be leading us on, because we heard it calling, deeper and deeper into the wood, and we went on and on, ending up in a kind of grassy enclosure, where we lay on our backs for a long time, staring up at the trees. Mathius thought he saw it. It was brilliant yellow, and we followed it to this place we found, because several times we heard it whistling, like a flute.'

'What luck!' I said. 'I envy you. Where you were is obviously its terrain. That's where I once thought I heard it.'

'Mathius and I are going to go there and see if we can spot the female, although it's not so striking, more a yellowish green.'

'And what about the young?'

'I don't suppose they'll be hanging around now. This is August, but Mathius has very good binoculars which he'll bring the next time.'

'We must get your photograph developed. I'll be going in tomorrow. I found a great shop, and they had espadrilles there which I'd like.'

'I've never heard you talking about clothes before.'

'Espadrilles are shoes, not clothes. I'll buy you a pair if you want to come with me.'

'No, thanks. They're no good for stalking. We're going tomorrow. But if I take out the film, will you have it developed when you go to Souillac?'

'OK.'

After our supper I went upstairs to do some work. I found it difficult to concentrate. Chantal's laughing glance kept flashing up in my mind. She was very attractive. Merle had rarely teased me, possibly because she accepted everything I said. Had she really felt that I was right all the time or had Margot said to her, 'Pretend, darling. Men like to be flattered'? Chantal would never be like that, I knew. She would disagree with me, and be very sure when she was right. I typed away, but after a time, I had to give it up. The house was quiet. The children must have gone to bed without saying goodnight to me. Of course Merle had always told them 'not to disturb Daddy', and perhaps they had decided to keep to that here.

I went downstairs and found a remarkably tidy kitchen. The table was quite clear. They knew how I hated to find crumbs on it, and one of them had wiped it clean. I could smell the ammoniac smell of cleaning liquid.

I went upstairs, and stood listening in the upstairs hall. There was a faint sound of music coming from Nick's room. I knocked, and he said, 'Declare yourself!'

'It's Dad,' I said.

'*Entrez.*'

'You've both popped off early tonight.'

'We didn't want to disturb you. Betsy was saying that we mustn't forget that you write for a living and . . .'

'We're not starving yet. I sold two books, if you remember, after Mummy died, and that will keep us going very well.'

'It must be quite worrying, though, when you know that you ought to be working instead of playing around here.'

'Oh, we can still afford holidays, Nick! You're right, though, writing is a rather precarious way of earning a living, not like other things. Law, for instance.'

'Do you think Madame Chantal is rolling in it?'

'I don't know. She may have some capital from her father, but she does have to work to keep up the château, and for people like her and myself, we have to think of education for the family. I would want you and Betsy to pursue anything you chose to study without having to worry about money.'

'Would Granny Strong not help there?'

'I shouldn't expect her to. She has paid for all your fees at school, but I don't see her going on with that, university fees and such like.'

'Betsy and I were just saying it must be miserable for you without Mummy to talk to.'

'It was at first, but I've been happy for quite a time, recently.'

He gave me what I can only call a searching look. 'We just wanted you to know that we think of you often, and when we leave school, we'll do our best not to be a burden to you.'

'You'll never be that, ' I said. 'Well, I'd better get off and leave you in peace.' I reached down and patted his shoulder. 'Good night, old son.' He was too big to hug.

Eleven

The next morning after a hurried breakfast, Betsy and Nick went off to the château, Nick to birdwatch with Mathius and Betsy to see Lenore's collection of earrings. I promised to go to Souillac and hand in Nick's film to be developed. I was as keen as he was to see it.

As I drove past the road to the mill, my mind filled with thoughts of Marie and Henri. Merle would have been really sorry, I thought, to know of the trouble they were in.

When I had parked the car in Souillac, I made my way to the shop where I had bought my jacket and trousers. I got a cheerful welcome from Marcel.

'*Bonjour*, Monsieur. How nice to see you again! What can I do for you?'

'It was those espadrilles you have in the window,' I said. 'I noticed them last time I was here. I wonder if you have my size?'

'We shall soon see.' He went away and came back with three boxes. 'Shall we try these for size? You seem to be replenishing your wardrobe these days, Monsieur?'

'*Pas du tout*,' I said. 'But there are some things I've run short of.'

'Ah, I see,' he said. 'Yvonne and I always say, in cases like yours, "*Cherchez la femme.*"' He gave me such a winning smile that I could not possibly take offence.

'It's strange,' I said, 'that one always seems to run out of several things at once.'

'*D'accord*,' he nodded.

One of the pairs he had brought was just the right fit, and as he was putting them into a carrier bag, he said, 'While

88

you're here, I have some nice linen trousers which would go well with them. The same colour?'

I shook my head, smilingly. 'No, thanks.'

His wife appeared as we were talking. 'How nice to see you again! But we always say that the lucky people who discover our shop soon return. *N'est-ce pas,* Marcel?'

'*C'est ça.* We are like a hidden jewel.' He proffered the carrier bag to me.

'Now you know where to come, Monsieur, should you require linen trousers.'

I got a brilliant send-off from them, having refused coffee. You can take a joke too far.

I decided to put my purchases in the car, take Nick's film to the pharmacist and then buy a paper to read while I was sitting having coffee. Next to me in the car park, I saw a woman stowing shopping in the boot of her car. When she looked up our eyes met. It was Marie Leroy. 'Marie!' I said. 'I'm so glad to see you. How are you?'

'Not so well, Mr Woodbridge.' She put her handkerchief to her eyes. 'You'll have heard . . . Forgive me, but the shock of seeing you . . .'

'Perhaps I've startled you. Why not join me for a cup of coffee? I'm on my way to have one.'

I saw her hesitate. 'It is too public here,' she said.

'Well, why don't I drive you to that hotel on the outskirts?'

'The Lion d'Or? I've left Thibaud with my mother. I mustn't be too long.'

'I understand. But I would like to have a chat with you and ask you about Henri. I have been thinking of both of you a lot. I am now established in Mr Maury's cottage.'

'*D'accord.*' She locked her car, and I drove her to the Lion d'Or, which was only about five minutes away.

When we had settled at a table in a dark corner that she chose, I did my best to put her at ease. 'My children are enjoying Bernay very much,' I said. 'They have made good friends with Lenore and Mathius at the château.'

'Ah, Madame Gibert will like that. She is attractive, don't you find? Henri always said that. When Henri and I worked there, he said how kind she was to her father when her

mother died. She gave up working in Paris to be beside him.'
Her look seemed to deprecate her words. Or was I mistaken?
And as if she wanted to disprove my suspicions, she went
on, 'And she helped Henri in buying the hotel, arranged a
loan for him.'

'Yes, I said, 'she has been very kind to us.' I was surprised
how my heart warmed at the thought of Chantal. 'Tell me,
Marie, are you allowed to see Henri?'

'Yes, he is in custody just now.' Her eyes filled with tears.
'Oh, Monsieur, if you knew how I've suffered . . .'

'I can imagine. Is there anything I can do to help?' She
shook her head and buried her face in her handkerchief.
'Come on, Marie, you mustn't distress yourself.' The waiter
was at my side. 'Two coffees, please,' I said, 'and two
brandies.' Marie still had her face buried in her handkerchief. I looked at her and then at the waiter. He nodded, as
if he understood. Perhaps he thought it was a lover's tiff.
She had recovered sufficiently when he returned to give him
a watery smile.

When he had gone, I said to her, 'Drink your brandy first,
Marie, it will help you.' I lifted my glass. 'Here's to a happy
outcome to your troubles.'

She lifted hers and clinked it with mine. 'You're so kind,
but perhaps if you knew what I've done, you wouldn't be
so kind. It was I who persuaded Henri to shoot Raymond.
I've thought of telling Madame Gibert because I know she
liked Henri, but I hadn't the same rapport with her that he
had.'

I spoke as calmly as I could. 'Would you like me to tell
her what is worrying you? I see her quite often. You can rest
assured that I wouldn't speak to anyone in the village.'

'I know I can trust you, Monsieur. I'm going mad living
with *Maman,* she keeps on prying, and says I shall have to
go soon, as she can't harbour Thibaud and me any more,
that the neighbours are talking.'

'I would do anything I could to help you and I know
Madame Gibert would too.'

'Henri is shielding me!' The words burst from her.

'Has he confessed to shooting . . .?' I stopped speaking,

because she gave a small moan as if she couldn't bear to hear Baron's name.

'Tell me, Marie,' I said. 'Are you protecting Raymond Baron?'

She looked at me, angrily. 'Raymond Baron! If you knew the fool he made of me, and how I detest him now! I was a stupid woman! He came to our hotel, Monsieur Woodbridge, because of the water failure. We both liked him and trusted him. Then, to my shame, I fell in love with him. We met many times in the afternoon without Henri's knowledge, sometimes in the wood beneath the *causse*, sometime in the ruined mill. When I told him I was pregnant and that the baby was his, he told me not to worry, that he would leave his wife and take me and Thibaud away. He kept saying this to me and doing nothing! When the baby was born and I knew it was his, I begged him to take us away. I was so ashamed. I told him that Henri suspected him. I don't know if he did, but he had certainly lost his trust in me. He humiliated me by making me parade Thibaud in front of the customers. I wrote to Raymond and told him this, and he promised that he would take us away the next time Henri sent for him to fix the water. He came eventually and that night Henri and I had a dreadful quarrel. "You see," he said, "the baby is his. Everybody is laughing at me!" He forced me to admit it. I said that I had fallen out of love with Raymond because of his broken promises. I begged him to forgive me, and said that I deeply regretted my behaviour. This was true, Monsieur. Have you ever known a state of mind where you realize you have been foolish and you have betrayed your partner?'

'I have to admit I haven't, but there are thousands who find themselves in that state and bitterly regret it.' I put my hand over her clasped ones on the table. 'So, did Henri forgive you?'

'Yes, but of course his anger turned on the Alsatian, as he called him. I suggested a plan of revenge to Henri. Oh, my God, what was I thinking of? Who could believe that I, an ordinary girl from a small town like this, would conceive of such a plan? I would arrange to meet Raymond in the mill, and I would say to him that I had left Thibaud in the car and I would go and get him. I would then stay in the car with the baby, while Henri would get out, creep up to the mill and shoot Raymond from the broken window of the room. Incredible, isn't it, Monsieur? It was a lie. I knew Raymond would never take me away, with or without the baby.'

I shook my head and said, 'Yes, it's difficult to believe.' And so it was. It was so French, I thought, a *crime passionel*. 'It all went according to plan,' she went on. 'I met Raymond at the mill, and I pretended to be glad that he had come to take me away. I said that I'd go to the car and get Thibaud. I knew by his expression that he had no intention of keeping his promise, but he let me go. I don't know what he intended to do if and when I returned with the baby, perhaps more promises, perhaps escape while I was away, perhaps kill us . . . he was a coward, Monsieur, a man who couldn't face up to his responsibilities. Of course I realized that far too late.

'When I got to the car I said to Henri, "Go on," and he got out of the car with his rifle. I heard the shot, and had to hush Thibaud because the noise frightened him and he started to cry. Henri was shaking when he came back to me. "I've done it," he said. "Remember, I've done it for you." He was still holding his rifle, and I said he would have to get rid of it. He said he knew just the place. I'll never forget that time. Thibaud crying in my arms, Henri away hiding the rifle, and the knowledge that Raymond was lying there dead.' She stopped speaking, put down her glass and buried her face in her hands. I comforted her, but at the same time I felt uneasy. Her description of what had happened seemed to come so easily, like something which had been rehearsed many times. But Baron was dead, Henri was in prison . . . She was speaking again. 'We drove back to the hotel, and I put Thibaud to bed. He was such a good baby! He was laughing all the time I bathed him. When Henri came to bed, he was so drunk he could hardly speak. "Remember," he said. "I did it for you."'

'How long had you to wait before the body was found?' I asked her.

'Oh, Monsieur, the longest time in my life! A friend of Raymond's with whom he shared duties on the water towers reported to the company that Raymond hadn't returned to their flat in Souillac. Evidently this friend knew of Raymond and me, he must have told him, and he reported his disappearance to the police. It didn't take them long to discover Raymond's body at the mill, and then they came one day to the hotel, and accused Henri of killing him. It was at least a week before they came to us, and then when they did, he confessed, and said he had shot Raymond Baron. I wept and protested, but they wouldn't listen to me, and he was taken away. Shall I ever forget his face? Believe me, Monsieur, I've wept ever since.'

I looked at her. She was deathly pale, and her eyes were swollen and red-rimmed, her hair lank. 'You poor soul,' I said. 'I'll tell Chantal what you've told me and we'll see if she can help you in any way.'

'Oh, thank you, thank you, Monsieur!' She grasped my hands. 'It's been such a relief unburdening myself. But you see what a good husband I have in Henri, and he's taken all the blame on his shoulders. Can you imagine how I suffer? Remorse! It bites deep in my heart. I am allowed to visit him, but he says he won't change his statement. I remember his words when we were at the mill that night. "I do this for you." I have asked to see someone in authority, but they dismiss my pleas.'

'I'll tell Chantal tonight,' I said. 'She is an advocate. She will be able to help you, I'm sure.'

I ran her back to her car, and the sight of her bowed figure inside it, starting the engine and looking up to wave to me as she drove away, was tragic.

To take my mind off what I'd been told by Marie, I went back to the pharmacist, and true to their promise they had my prints ready. I sat in the car, staring at Nick's fine photograph of a golden oriole, with its slashed black wings and black tail. A handsome bird, I thought. Raymond Baron had been handsome too.

Twelve

After a time I drove back to Bernay. I remembered Merle's reaction when we had gone to the mill with Henri, and how we had both felt the same in the caves. The area was beautiful, but we had both felt the undercurrent of . . . something we couldn't put a name to. 'Eerie,' Merle had said. I searched for a simile, like a rose, worm-eaten in the centre. Something good had to happen to me to get rid of the feeling.

Betsy and Nick arrived a few minutes after me, their hair wet, and chattering away about the good time they'd had. Madame Gibert had given them lunch when the boys came back from birdwatching, and then they had all swum. Madame Gibert was such a good swimmer, and such fun . . . My spirits were raised by their happiness, and when I showed Nick his photograph, he was delighted. 'It's good, Dad. We were lucky today, too, at the same place. I think it haunts it. When we were walking along the track just before you come to this grassy enclosure – a great place for a picnic, we thought – there it was, standing in the middle of it. I didn't get a shot this time. We must have made a noise, because it suddenly flew upwards. We were able to see what looked like the remains of its nest this time, slung between two branches. We didn't see any signs of the female. But she's not nearly so dashing, poor thing.'

'Lenore's earrings are so pretty, Daddy. I'm going to ask for a pair on every birthday so that I have a collection like hers.'

'I take the hint,' I said. 'Look kids, I was thinking, driving home, Madame Gibert has been so kind to us, with the use of the swimming pool and everything. I'm going to ask her out to dinner, tonight, if possible.'

Two po-faces looked at me. 'Good idea,' Nick said.

'Did you bring us something to cook from Souillac?' Betsy said.

'Yes, one of those delicious quiche lorraines from the delicatessen. But first of all, I'll see if she's free.'

I went upstairs to my study. I didn't want the two of them within listening distance, their ears cocked. Chantal answered the telephone. '*Allô*!' I was beginning to love that greeting.

'Chantal,' I said. 'I have a surprise for you. I met Marie Leroy in Souillac today. She confided in me. I'd like to tell you what she said. Would you have dinner with me tonight? Just the two of us. I don't want the children to know of my meeting with Marie Leroy.'

'I understand. Yes, thank you,' she said. 'I know a good place on the other side of the valley. I can show you the way.'

'Splendid! And thank you for your hospitality to them today. They had a great time.'

'I love Betsy and Nick,' she said. 'The four of them are like a family to me.'

'Say, in half an hour?' I said. 'I'll call for you.'

'I'll be ready.'

She was wearing a flowered chiffon dress, which seemed to swirl about her legs as she got into the car. 'I thought you only wore black or white,' I said.

'Most of the time. This is a party dress.'

'It's very becoming,' I said. 'I'm wearing espadrilles I bought in Souillac today.'

'So?' she said.

'It's rare for me to talk about, or notice, clothes, or shoes. I don't know what's happening to me.' I remembered Marcel's quip, but couldn't say that.

'Maybe you're finding another Martin here,' she said. I glanced at her. Her eyes were laughing at me.

'You enjoy teasing me, don't you?'

'You're very teaseable. Perhaps your eyes have been opened since you came to Bernay.'

'It's certainly won me over.'

'We shan't talk about Marie until we arrive. Meantime I shall direct you to the restaurant. Now, this is the vale we're in. There is a scenic spot we're coming to soon, where I'm going to ask you to stop. I always do when I'm driving. It is breathtaking, and I stow it away in my mind for taking out and remembering when I'm in Paris. Here we are, this lay-by.'

We had driven through a pretty village, and after passing the row of cottages of that golden stone peculiar to the south-west of France, we had emerged to a view such as I had never seen in all my life. As far as the eye could reach, there was pasture land, bisected by hedges, trees shielding farm-houses, and beyond that a panorama that faded into a rosy pinkness of hills, which were difficult to trace because of the grey mist seemingly draped over them. We stood together, while Chantal pointed out to me landmarks which she recog-nized, mostly churches, their square towers surrounded by small clusters of houses. 'It's glorious,' I said. 'That's France to me.' I had put my arm round her waist quite naturally. 'I could imagine the sea is on the horizon.' I waved my hand.

'No,' she said. 'That is the only disadvantage. No sea. We have to be content with a pool. Now, I think we'd better push on. "Push on"? Yes? The place I'm taking you to gets quite busy.'

It was, and very smart. 'Where do all those people come from?' I asked Chantal when we'd been shown to a table *en plein air* in a paved alcove above a noisy stream. The sun was still hot, but fortunately there was an umbrella over the table. A waiter seated us, gave us a menu each, and asked about wine.

'I've got a lot to celebrate tonight,' I said to Chantal. 'Do you like champagne?'

'Who doesn't?'

She smiled at me and I noticed the flowered dress had a décollecté neckline and that she was wearing swinging earrings. I tried to prevent my eyes swinging like the earrings. Did she collect them too?

'What have you to celebrate?' she asked me. Her eyes were on mine, and she was smiling.

'My espadrilles,' I said, 'which I bought today. Something has come over me. I'm always buying for myself.'

'Are you trying to impress someone?' she asked me.

'I'm not aware that I am. But the shopkeeper made a similar remark. He said, "*Cherchez la femme*."' There, I'd said it.

'And have you?'

'I think so.'

The waiter returned with the champagne in an ice bucket and went through the usual ritual. When we each had our glasses filled, I raised mine. 'This is a momentous dinner, Chantal, for me.'

'*Bon*, but first of all, you have to tell me what Marie told you today.'

'Yes, of course.' Was she still teasing me?

I told her what Marie had confessed to me, and that I had said she could perhaps help her. Her eyes changed, as if she was assessing, thinking like an *avocat*.

'That would be difficult for me. It's a small world, the legal world. I might know who's representing her. But I'll speak to Detective Inspector Galimard when he comes to see me.'

'Have you any opinions of your own?' I asked her.

'Just opinions. The Henri I knew was a good lad, well known in the village. He had been brought up by an aunt, and she had taught him to be helpful. But that was his nature in any case. When he came to work for my father, he was an excellent worker and well liked. Then the trouble began when Marie was engaged as a parlour maid. He fell madly in love with her, and his whole attitude seemed to change. The hotel was up for sale, and she wanted him to buy it. She pushed him into asking my father for a loan, but he was old at the time, and couldn't deal with such a request. He told me, I was in Paris, and I came home. I saw Henri, and what a difference! He had changed from being a gentle lad to being an aggressive one. The staff were complaining about his behaviour, and blaming Marie. He asked me for a loan. "I feel I've worked here long enough to deserve it," he said. That wasn't Henri speaking, it was Marie. I said I could arrange a loan for him, which I did, and he and Marie moved into the hotel. It left my father without much help, but they

never apologized for that. Well, they ran the hotel success-
fully, until this engineer came along, and then things began
to go badly wrong. There were complaints from various local
people who dealt with them, about slipshod service, and
constant quarrels, and so on. Of course, there were rumours
in the village when the baby came along. I spoke to Henri
once when I was at the hotel and warned him that he was
losing custom. He said that he wasn't bothered about that,
that Marie wanted to entice foreigners to his hotel, not local
people. They had great plans for it.'

'We've talked and talked about the Leroys,' I said, looking
around. 'I think we're the only people here. The place is
deserted.'

She glanced at the empty tables. 'So it is,' she laughed.
'Had you something else to say?' Her eyes were on me again,
teasing.

'Yes, I had.' That damned waiter appeared at my side
again, and laid the bill in a saucer in front of me. While I
was paying it, I looked up and said to Chantal, 'I hope the
children are all right.' I thought he looked critically at us as
he lifted the saucer with the money on it. 'We'd better get
going,' I added.

'Don't worry about them,' Chantal said, making matters
worse, I thought. 'They can look after themselves.'

Driving back through the dark countryside, we hardly
spoke. At one point I said to her, 'We've exhausted ourselves
talking about the Leroys.' The champagne had been my friend.
I had been going to say how much I had enjoyed myself,
and lead up to . . . now I didn't know what I had been going
to lead up to.

'Not quite,' she said, putting her hand over mine on the
gear lever. 'We must hope for the best for the Leroys, but if
he's convicted, it will be a tragedy.'

'You're convinced she influenced him?' This was not what
I had been going to say at all.

'Yes, unfortunately. I think I'm more worldly wise than
you, Martin, even although you are a writer.'

'Writers can be psychiatrists. But from what you tell me,
it sounds as if he was hopelessly influenced by Marie. It's

not the first time that kind of thing has happened.' I couldn't get off the subject of the Leroys.

'Do you think you could be easily influenced?'

I was surprised at the question. 'On the surface, yes, but I'm not hasty. I turn things over in my mind.'

'Such as?' Her voice was soft.

'Sometimes I think I've fallen in love with you, and then I think it can't possibly be so. There was Merle. We had a happy marriage . . .'

'But you influenced her.'

'I suppose I did.'

'And you don't like the thought of being influenced.'

'Who by?'

'Any woman. Me, for instance.'

'It has never occurred to me. I don't mean being married to you, but being influenced.'

'It would be a change, perhaps?'

'I think of marriage as being two equal partners.'

'I think of marriage of, say, divided into eighths. What does it matter if one person provides five eighths and the other three eighths? As long as it makes a whole.'

I considered this. 'What was it like with your former husband?'

'The balance was wrong. He wanted to provide eight eighths. There was no room for me in it.'

'I see. With Merle, I suppose I provided six eights, which was how she liked it. She thought that was the norm in marriages.'

'Perhaps. But we're talking about happy marriages.'

'Ours was.'

'Of course you would say that. You were . . . top dog, is it?'

Her pronunciation of the words was so peculiar that it made me laugh.

'Why do you laugh, Martin?'

'I don't know. Just that you make me laugh.' Merle never made me laugh, I thought, she was too gentle. I found myself thinking that I would like a change, this time. 'Do you think it's too soon to propose to you?' I asked.

'Propose what?'

'Marriage.'

'Ah, yes, marriage. It's not too soon if your mind is clear that that is what you want to do.'

I acted on impulse, and drew into a convenient *aire de repos*, a comfortable lay-by unique to France. I took her in my arms. 'A resting place,' I said.

'Martin,' she said, 'what is this?'

'It's a proposal of marriage. There are heaps of things to discuss about the idea, but what do you think of it as an idea?'

'As a proposal you've made the right move. Why don't you kiss me?'

'I was just going to.'

It was a funny thing to be kissing someone who wasn't Merle, but it was delightful and exciting, and utterly different.

'Will you marry me?' I said.

'Englishman are so keen to put everything in order. "Yes," if that's what you want me to say. How do you like it?'

'Like what?'

'This?' She put her hands to the back of my neck and kissed me.

'I like it.'

'Well, let us stay here and enjoy ourselves, and forget about the children. And please don't let us have any sensible discussions. I know you're going to say sensible things, but I don't want to hear them. I just want to be happy.'

'I'll make you happy,' I said. We made each other happy.

I crept into the cottage like a burglar. I wondered if Betsy and Nick were listening to me, but there was no sound from their bedrooms. Chantal had gone tiptoe into the château when I dropped her. 'The children,' she said, her finger to her lips. 'That's another thing we didn't discuss.'

'Yes,' I whispered. 'We'll talk about it later.'

Bernay was seemingly not disturbed by Chantal and me creeping into our respective houses, like burglars. It lay peacefully asleep, and soon I sunk into its arms and was the same.

Thirteen

The three of us were sitting having breakfast the following morning. 'Did you enjoy yourself last night, Dad?' Nick asked.

'Yes, thank you,' I said.

'He's blushing,' Betsy said.

'Don't be ridiculous,' I said, thinking how Merle would have kept her in check. But that was a ridiculous thought, I realized.

'Lenore thinks it would be a good thing if you two got married,' she said. 'It would suit Nick and me very well. We could swim in the pool whenever we liked then.'

'Betsy!' Nick said, glancing at me apologetically.

'It's all right, Nick,' I said, wanting to add that I could fight my own battles, then deciding against it.

Betsy jumped up from her seat. 'Here's the postman!' She went dashing to the door and returned with a square envelope. 'It's addressed to you, Daddy.'

'Thanks.' I tore it open. I knew what it was, because Chantal had warned me last night. I read the words on the card inside out loud for their benefit. 'Madame Chantal Gibert requests the company of Monsieur Woodbridge and family to a poolside party on Saturday the twenty-sixth of August, 1967, at four p.m. to seven p.m. at the Château Bernay. RSVP. Do you two want to go?' I asked them.

'Of course we do,' Betsy said, outraged. 'We knew already. Lenore and Mathius told us yesterday.'

'Well, I'll reply for all of us,' I said. I went up to my study, telling them I was going to work until lunchtime, and immediately dialled Chantal.

'*Allô*,' I heard her voice.

'How are you?'

'Marvellous. How are you?'

'Marvellous. Your invitation came.'

'Good.'

'I'm getting some cheek from Betsy.'

'What about?'

'You and me.'

'She needs to be taught decorum. Lenore wouldn't dare, although I know she's dying to make some comment. We'll take them a picnic to the *causse* tomorrow. It's a favourite place of ours for picnics.' It used to be a favourite place of Merle's and mine too, I thought, but it all seemed far enough away. Merle would be happy for me. I raised my eyebrows at the thought.

We arranged the time for the picnic, and I took Betsy and Nick to Souillac for lunch. I hoped we wouldn't meet Marie Leroy, and, fortunately, we didn't.

They had never been to Pech Merle, the cave near the Cele river, and I suggested we might go there. 'It must be one of the finest painted caves in France, except Lascaux,' I told them. 'Do you remember me telling you of having visited Lascaux with my parents when I was about Nick's age? I was lucky to have seen it because it had to be closed in 1963. The number of people visiting it was slowly ruining it. Sweat and breath went for the paintings. It was having seen it which inspired me later on to push further into the Lot where I knew there might be other caves because of the limestone. I've been coming back since then because I fell in love with the region.' I stopped speaking because I saw *that* look on their faces: 'He's off again . . .' 'Anyhow,' I said, 'it's worth you two keeping your eyes open, because it was four boys who discovered Lascaux. They were out looking for treasure with their dog when it ran down what at first they thought was a rabbit-hole but turned out to be the entrance to the cave.'

We set off after lunch, with little enthusiasm on the children's part. The thought of the picnic tomorrow to the *causse*, however, seemed to please them, and we had bought pâté de foie, little pies filled with salmon, and some *pâtisseries* in

Souillac. Chantal had said she would make sandwiches and bring soft drinks, and I could provide wine for us, if I wished.

However, once we were on the N20 and speeding along, they stopped talking about the picnic, and began to ask questions about Pech Merle.

'It is huge,' I told them, 'and it's been likened to a Sistine chapel. It's *amenagée*, there are hand-rails provided, because the floor's often wet and slippy, so look out.'

When we went in, they were immediately silenced by the atmosphere, I don't know quite how to describe it, as if we had stepped back in time. Anyone with a scrap of imagination is bound to feel in touch with their ancestors, these Paleolithic men who roamed this region forty thousand years ago. The children were fascinated by the paintings, especially the dappled horses, and the thought of them having been drawn by Stone Age man silenced them. They were in awe, and wanted to know all sorts of things, when these men had lived, why were some animals drawn sideways on; 'twisted perspective' is the name used, I told them, and I noticed that, like at Rocamadour, they were beginning to get the feel of the region, just as I had as a boy, its beauty above and its mystery below. I bought them books that they could read at home, and pointed out to them that the limestone was the key to those caves, because it was porous and let water soak through very easily, which accounted for the stalactites and stalagmites which they had seen.

Nick said, when we went back to the car, 'It's like being in a different world. I can imagine those Stone Age men, and how some of them must have been gifted, like a boy in my class at school, Robin Craig. Our form master, Mr Meldrum, always says Robin is lucky because he's gifted.'

Betsy had her own thoughts. 'I never get this feeling in Kent.'

'It's a kind of timelessness,' I said.

'Of knowing your place in the queue,' Nick said. I was pleased that my son was getting the hang of it.

'Right, Nick,' I said, and risking being pedantic, 'a question of understanding your place in the development of man from the Paleolithic times to us in the twentieth century.'

'Think if we'd been first or second in the queue,' Betsy said, 'we could have been dressed in bearskins,'

'And wearing bone earrings,' I said.

'And sitting at a fire, sharpening flints,' Nick offered.

'And babies crawling about dressed in baby bearskins.'

Their imaginations kept them busy as I drove back along the N20 and on to the side road, passing the place Chantal and I had stood to see the view. I was happy at that moment, happy with my children, who I thought were pretty good, happy at the thought of the future, a general happiness that I didn't want to explore further.

When we got home, we joked and laughed in the kitchen, shambling about like bears. We packed away the picnic goodies in the fridge, and Betsy looked out cutlery and plates and glasses and put them in a box for tomorrow. Nick was sorry we'd forgotten paper napkins, but I assured him that Chantal would no doubt provide them.

'With crests on them,' Nick said.

It had been a happy day.

Fourteen

The day dawned misty, but with the promise of brightening up later, and we drove up to the meeting place I had arranged with Chantal, at the church where the path to the *causse* began. The Giberts arrived shortly after us, and they had a carrier on wheels with them in which to stow the picnic stuff. We left the cars in the church car park.

We set off up the path, the children ahead of Chantal and myself. I felt ridiculously happy to see her, and I was torn between the wish to keep looking at her and the wish not to be seen doing so by Betsy and Nick. I had never thought the day would come when they would embarrass me.

Chantal said, her voice low, 'Remember the *aire de repos*?'

'Shall I ever forget it?' I felt I was leering like a schoolboy.

'Don't look at me like that. You'll embarrass me.'

'I'll try not to. Yes, I remember the *aire de repos*.'

'Well, near it there is a field with a dolmen in it, I thought Betsy and Nick would like to see it. It's a favourite place of ours.'

'The field is really part of the *causse*?'

'Certainly. You'll see that if we go there, it is plateau land, not pasture.'

'I certainly would like to see it. This is good. We have our own dolmen!' I was grateful for her suggestion. If we went on further, where Merle and I had been in the habit of going, she was bound to be in my mind.,

'I took my two to Pech Merle yesterday, they've either had enough of prehistoric times or they'll be thirsting for more.'

'Let's ask them.'

'Hi!' I shouted. 'Come back! We have something to discuss.'

They did. I noticed Betsy and Lenore were sharing the pushing of the carrier.

The four of them stopped beside Chantal and me with blank faces. 'We're coming to the field where the dolmen is.' she said. 'Lenore and Mathius know it. Are you two, Betsy and Nick, interested in seeing it?'

'What's a dolmen?' they said in unison.

'Historians think it was used as a burial place, or marked a burial place. There are hundreds all over the Lot, but we're lucky to have this one near us. It's in a field beyond here and we can easily get into it by pushing through a gap in the hedge.'

'We call it our very own dolmen,' Mathius said. 'We used to have great picnics in the field where it is.'

'Well, what are we waiting for?' Nick said.

'Then you boys can be in charge of the picnic stuff,' Lenore said. 'Betsy and I have pushed it far enough.'

'OK,' Nick said. 'Let's go.' He took the handle of the carrier and began pushing it along the path. 'Come on, Mathius.'.

'Yes, you go with Nick,' Chantal said to Mathius, 'and show him where to go through.'

In a few minutes we were settled beside the dolmen in a wild meadow, definitely *causse* land, which fortunately had not been ploughed. There were enough flowers there to gladden our hearts, and the smell of thyme.

'Well, what do you think of the dolmen?' Chantal said, pointing to the two standing stones with a stone slab resting on them.

'I'm just wondering how they heaved that stone across the two standing ones,' Nick said.

'And why?' Mathius added.

'Don't you remember we decided there must be a mathematical reason behind it?' his mother said. 'And that they calculated the setting sun would shine through the aperture?'

'It would require a lot of calculation,' I said. 'But that's one theory.'

'We have grandad's books at the château. We'll look them up. What do you say, Nick?'

'Oh, yes, please!' Nick said. She's won him over too, I thought.

After we had our picnic, the children began a game of cricket, and Chantal and I took a walk round the meadow. The view was certainly almost as good as higher up the *causse*. 'It's a wonderful feeling,' I said to her. 'As if one were on top of the world. This may be tactless, Chantal, but I used to walk to the *causse* with Merle, and I think of her now with a certain sadness.'

'And perhaps inevitability. Time moves on, and one moves with it. I have not the same feelings about my former husband, but since I met you I can think of him with kindness, and not bitterness. Kindness is better to live with than bitterness. And, after all, he gave me two children whom I love.'

'You're wise as well as beautiful,' I said. 'Are you still going to marry me? I know Betsy and Nick would approve.'

'And so would Mathius and Lenore. I think they're getting impatient with us.'

'And I feel I'm being precipitate.'

'Why?'

'Well, you have a lovely house, and I only have two cottages.'

'And I possibly earn more money than you?' Is that another worry?'

'These are two important things.'

'Well, if it helps, I'll tell you that I intend to retire at forty. I'm tired of life in Paris. So there would only be a few years, then you would have to take us over. Does that help?'

'It takes care of the mundane things, which don't really matter. So, until you retire, would we see enough of each other?'

'Your work enables you to live anywhere you like. What's wrong with you being here, or in Paris?'

'Nothing, nothing at all. This all seems too sensible, but then, neither of us are very young. So far, we've discussed my side of things. What about you? Would you like Lenore and Mathius to regard me as a stepfather? Would you like to be married to a writer, a mediocre one?'

'Martin,' she laughed. 'You are altogether too pedantic.

We love each other. You proved that to me coming back from dinner that night. That is sufficient for me. I knew when I met you that day about the cottage that I could love you. I'm very sure of myself. My work has trained me. I can look forward to you and the four children, and a beautiful life in the château, watching them grow up, and in time they'll marry and we'll have them and their wives and families to stay. I've not had a happy life. I know I'm capable of it. You've had a happy life with Merle. But this will be a different kind of happiness for you, a wiser kind. I think the future looks good for us.'

'And if you allow Betsy and Nick to swim in your pool, they'll thoroughly approve of you and me joining up.' I laughed.

'I've a feeling the four of them will be quite pleased with the situation. Are you old-fashioned, Martin?'

'In what way?'

'Need we marry?'

'Anything will suit me, as long as we can sleep together.'

'We can start any time.'

'That's good to know, but families can be in the way, sometimes.'

When we got back to the children, they were sitting on the grass. The game had finished. 'Have you all worked out the purpose of the dolmen?' I asked them.

'We know it was a burial place for the people who lived here thousands of years ago. Mathius has read it up,' Nick said. There was a pause. Chantal and I exchanged glances.

'I have to ask you, Mathius and Lenore,' I said. 'If Chantal and I got married, would you mind if Betsy, Nick and myself came to live with you? And, of course, you're more than welcome to come and live with us in England.' I was working out, as I spoke, how many bedrooms our house had in Kent. But, of course, I could sell it and the cottage here, which would enable me to buy a bigger house.

There was a moment's silence. Then they looked at each other and smiled.

'It sounds a great idea,' Betsy said. 'Lenore and I have only quarrelled once.'

'Mathius and I don't quarrel,' Nick said. 'We work things out.'

'Would you wear a wedding dress and a veil, *Maman*, when you and Martin get married?' Lenore asked.

'I hadn't thought of it, *cherie*,' Chantal said. 'I don't think it matters.'

'I think you two getting married is a great idea,' Mathius said. The other three looked at him with approval.

When we were all walking back to the cars, I could see that the children were turning over in their minds this latest development in their lives, now that it was out in the open. They had gone silent. I looked at Chantal, and she seemed to feel the same thing, because she nodded and said, 'Look, the sun is shining. Isn't that good? Why don't we all hurry home and get into swimsuits and have some fun in the pool?'

'Great!' Mathius said. It seemed to have become his favourite word. In fact, the four spoke a polyglot language which both parties had made peculiarly their own. I wondered if, when they grew up, this would continue. It was another interesting facet of this new venture I was going to make.

Chantal's idea was a good one. We had competitions in the pool, who could swim underwater for the longest time, who could lift a coin from the bottom first, and races. Chantal impressed me. She beat the girls, and came second to Mathius. She was full of surprises.

I took them all to dinner at the restaurant where Chantal and I had dined, and the children surprised us in what they packed away. 'Good thing we didn't have to slay a few animals for our dinner,' Nick said. He must have seen the bill.

'Like the Stone Age people, you mean,' Mathius said.

'Nor lift a huge slab of stone for the crossbar of a dolmen,' I said.

'We should be too busy to help you,' Lenore said, 'minding the babies.'

'Or sewing bearskin vests,' Betsy said.

I felt quite bucolic and parental, and judging by Chantal's expression, she was in some kind of happy fugue. The only drawback was that having four children swarming around us, we didn't know how we could get together, but she sat beside me when I was driving back and put her hand over mine on the gear lever, and that was enough.

So I thought, had Mathius not said to Nick in a voice that was meant to be heard, 'Don't they ever kiss?'

Fifteen

The day of the pool party dawned, and Betsy and Nick were away early, as they had to help with blowing up balloons and placing chairs round the pool and generally helping to create a party atmosphere. I followed shortly afterwards and found Chantal in the kitchen with the Vilars, organizing the food. 'Hello!' she said when I appeared. 'Just in time. Madame Vilar and I have the food ready, as you see. You go with Monsieur and attend to the liquid refreshment.'

I saluted, 'Certainly, Madame Gibert.'

'Go on, stupid,' she said to me, putting an arm round my neck and kissing me.

I saw the Vilars exchanging glances, but I was so happy I didn't mind.

We all worked hard, and at lunchtime we had an al fresco lunch in the kitchen and a glass of well-earned wine.

The children went away to change into their swimsuits, but Chantal and I remained as we were, ready to receive guests. They began to arrive at four o'clock, and I noticed she had invited most of the village people. 'My father always had a garden party each year for the village, so this is just the same, with the addition of the pool,' she explained. The neighbours arrived first, a bevy of chattering, well-dressed people, but the only ones I knew were Madame and Monsieur Lavare, she of the blue swimsuit I had seen before (or perhaps she always wore blue to match her eyes) and a sarong in brilliant colours tied round her waist, all topped with an immense straw hat. Both she and her husband greeted me enthusiastically, Monsieur Lavare with, I thought, knowing looks, because Chantal had said, 'And you remember Martin, don't you? I don't know what I'd do without him.'

111

'How convenient for you, Chantal,' Ana Lavare said. 'But then you always have someone in tow.'

Suddenly, it seemed the gardens were full of people and children. I recognized Guy Rosier with his wife, and I said to Chantal, 'Where do they all come from, apart from the villagers?'

'Some from Paris,' she said, 'and some from big houses around here. You never see them, because like us they are busy entertaining or being entertained. And the ladies play bridge in the afternoons. And soon we'll have the hunting season.'

'I remember Henri saying to me he intended to keep the hotel going until the hunters came. It makes me think that at that time he had no plans to get rid of Baron.'

'Which makes you think that Marie influenced him?'

'Yes. You said you had invited Detective Inspector Galimard. Is he here?'

She looked around. 'Yes, there he is, talking to Phillipe D'Erlanger. But you don't know him. We were very friendly when I was eighteen.'

'You're trying to make me jealous.'

'Yes, it's natural, *cheri*.' Merle never flirted, and so I had never been jealous of her. I must stop those comparisons.

We watched Galimard looking around, catching sight of Chantal, then speaking to this former – boyfriend? lover? – of Chantal's. I wondered. 'He's coming to speak to us,' Chantal said.

The detective had evidently made his excuses because he came striding towards us.

'Ah, Monsieur Galimard.' Chantal gave him a brilliant smile. 'How nice to see you. But where is your wife?'

'She sends her apologies, Madame, but she didn't feel well this morning. The journey, you understand . . .'

'Of course. But did you feel like coming alone?'

'I had said to you I would come today and see you and Mr Woodbridge. I wanted to keep that promise. Besides, Charlotte insisted that I come here.' He lowered his voice, and said, bashfully, *'En fait, elle est enceinte.'* He included me in his announcement.

112

'*Ah, mes félicitations! Comme vous serez heureux!*' Chantal said.

I saw the detective inspector change to a sheepishly happy man.

'My congratulations,' I said, holding out my hand. I was with Chantal on her reaction: the news that his wife was pregnant was happy indeed.

'*Merci,* Monsieur. Now we mustn't let my happy news interfere with our affairs. Is there somewhere we can talk, Madame?'

'Let's all go into the house. Monsieur Woodbridge is now my fiancé, Monsieur.'

'Now it is my turn to offer my felicitations!' He smiled at us, and we both beamed back.

She led the way up the steps from the pool, bowing and smiling to various people in our path, and the detective and I followed. We all sat down in the drawing room, and Chantal said, 'Martin, if you would pour some wine for us.'

'Certainly.' Monsieur Galimard didn't refuse when I gave him a glass of wine. I wondered if a detective in England would have accepted it, but when in Rome, I thought, and helped Chantal and myself to the same.

'And what is the news of Henri?' she asked him.

'He's still in custody. His trial may not take place for some time, I'm afraid.'

'Poor Henri. I told you what Mr Woodbridge had told me of his meeting with Marie.'

'Yes, you did, and I should like to question you about that meeting, sir. Did you form the impression that she was sincere, that she was telling the truth?'

'Yes, I think so.' I cast my mind back. Perhaps it had been strange that she had unburdened herself to me? Had she prepared her story already, and it just happened that we met, and she could try it out on me? 'She did seem very upset. She was crying.'

'Some women can cry to order. I have interviewed her, and she has told me the same story, that she suggested to her husband that he should shoot her lover. And that she was the decoy.'

'That is what she told me. I had no reason to disbelieve her.'

'You're an *avocat*, Madame Gibert, how does this information strike you?'

'Well, of course, I haven't seen her, but I got to know her and Henri very well when they worked for my father. She had a great influence on Henri, and I know it was she who suggested he should ask for a loan from my father to buy the hotel.'

'I've made enquiries in Souillac where she worked before coming to the château here, and she was known by her fellow workmates as an ambitious girl. The women didn't like her, but the men were, well, you know, appreciative. I got the impression that she had been –' he hesitated – 'liked better by the men.'

'That gives one the impression of a *femme fatale*,' Chantal said.

'Correct. I'm going to see the *avocat* who is representing Henri.' Galimard turned to me. 'I'd like you to swear to an affidavit for me, Monsieur. It would mean you coming to my office in Cahors where your statement will be taken down, then you'll be asked to sign it. It will be presented to the *avocat* dealing with her case. At the moment I don't know where the court will sit, possibly Cahors, but I'll keep in touch with either you or Madame Gibert and let you know.'

'I feel I should tell you, Monsieur Galimard,' Chantal said, 'that Monsieur Woodbridge and I will be taking up residence together soon. So we can be reached at this address.'

'Quite,' the man said. 'Congratulations are due, then.' He beamed on both of us.

'We'll be married soon, of course,' I said. I didn't like this 'taking up residence soon' at all. I intended to tell Chantal.

'I hope you will be as happy as I and my dear Charlotte are,' he said. He was a genuine chap – for a detective.

He took his leave then, giving me his card with his address, and excusing himself from the official opening of the pool because of his dear Charlotte.

When he had gone, Chantal said to me, 'Was that you being masterful?'

'Yes,' I said. 'Don't you like it?'

'I adore it,' she said. 'You are unique, my darling.'

We had a little time together before we mingled with the rest of the party. Quite a few of the guests were already in the pool, and Chantal made a little speech welcoming everyone. Our children cut free all the balloons and they drifted over the pool, while the guests were served with aperitifs and food. 'I also have a little announcement to make,' she said, 'to all my friends here and those in Bernay. Monsieur Woodbridge, here beside me, and I, are affianced and will be married shortly. We'd like you to drink to our health and happiness.'

We were immediately surrounded by people wishing to shake our hands or kiss us, a positive mêlée, I thought. Guy Rosier came up to me and shook my hand vigorously. 'Congratulations!' he said. 'We couldn't have anyone better in the château than you. The old count would have been very pleased.'

'Thank you, Guy,' I said. 'I shall be happy to be accepted by Bernay.'

When I and the children trailed home about nine o'clock, we were too happy to speak. At least I was.

Their happiness was more vocal. 'Madame Gibert said to us she was looking forward to having a big family,' Betsy said.

Nick said judiciously. 'Mathius and I took to each other right away.'

Sixteen

I telephoned the police department in Cahors and made an appointment to see Galimard. I drove through to Cahors on my own, parking, with some difficulty, near the Boulevard Gambetta and my favourite café, where I enjoyed a coffee and some people-watching. Detective Galimard's office was near the Pont Valentré, and I couldn't resist walking along it in the sunshine. It always seems hotter in Cahors, a step further to the south. I had a photograph of Merle at home, standing on this impressive bridge, with the Devil's Tower in the background. She had been like a child, I thought, always having to walk over any bridge we came across, and she had been fascinated by the legend of Lucifer and the master mason in the case of the Pont Valentré. I couldn't remember the details as I stood looking at the Lot flowing under it, except that it concerned a pact between the devil and the mason, and how the latter had ousted the devil by sending him to fetch water in a sieve! Her delight in the story had been that of a little girl's. But Chantal is a woman, I thought . . .

I spoke to myself. Will you be able to stop thinking of Merle when you're married to Chantal? I love her, and want to be with her, but is it usual to think often of your former wife? What do other men do in my situation?

Get on with it, of course. It was surely to be expected that when one had lived with a woman for about seventeen years, one couldn't dismiss her from one's life. She had been part of it. We had had two children. You think too much, Martin, I told myself. Go by your feelings, not your memories. There on the Pont Valentré the solution came to me. Stop dismissing her from your mind, but get on with your life. It stretches ahead of you, inviting. You're a lucky chap to meet someone so soon whom you would like to live with, someone who wanted to be a mother to your children.

I met Galimard, feeling good, and glad I had settled my mind. The detective inspector was very welcoming. I enquired about his wife, and his face softened as he told me she was very well. 'People tell me the first three months are the worst,' he said.

I agreed. 'I remember my wife was sick to begin with,' I told him, 'but she felt really well after that.'

Having compared notes, he said to me, 'Now to business. I would like you to speak into this tape recorder, repeating everything that Marie Leroy told you.'

I did this, wondering again if I'd been duped, and when I indicated that I had finished, he rang the bell on his desk. A young officer appeared. 'Please have this typed right away,' Galimard said, 'and bring it back to me.' When the man had gone out, he looked at me. 'I hope you aren't in a hurry, Mr Woodbridge, but this procedure is necessary.'

'Not at all,' I said. 'I'm enjoying revisiting your beautiful city.'

'You've seen our old *quartier*, *les Badernes*, with our wonderful cathedral?' he asked.

'Yes,' I said. 'Long ago with my wife.' I spoke without a qualm. ' I've come alone today. Madame Gibert was taking the children to Souillac. We all go back home at the end of the month.'

'You to England and she to Paris? Well, of course, she is a busy woman. I congratulate you, Mr Woodbridge. She is highly thought of, as was her father.'

The door opened, and a woman officer came in with two cups of coffee on a tray. 'Thank you,' he said to her, and to me, 'I trust you will join me in my morning coffee.'

'Thank you,' I said.

'You are a true Frenchman, Mr Woodbridge,' he smiled, leaning back in his chair.'I can tell you, sir, regarding this case of the Leroys, that Madame Gibert was first choice for the defendant, but she refused because she had known both parties.'

'We're both very interested in the case. Will Marie's confession make any difference?'

'I think you asked me that before. Who knows? It's true to say that in the eighteenth century, *crime passionel* was accepted as an excuse, but not now. However, when the judge knows the details it might make a difference. I should say it depends on the judge.'

'In a way it can be no longer called a *crime passionnel* because of Marie's confession.'

'Perhaps, but that's splitting hairs. However, time will tell.' He sighed. 'I see all variations of the human condition in my job. I sometimes think I've become something of a philosopher.' He squared with his hands some papers on his desk. 'But I am obliged to submit your affidavit, as part of the case. It's doubtful if she's helped her husband by this confession.'

'My father used to say to me, "Truth stands all investigation," and one must abide by that.' There was a knock at the door, and the officer came in and handed the typed affidavit to Galimard. He read it through, and held it out to me.

'If you would check that and sign if you're happy with it, Mr Woodbridge.'

I did this, and handed it back.

'Thank you,' he said. 'And may I wish you every happiness in your future life with Madame Gibert. I have no doubt it will be a happy one.'

We shook hands, and I drove back full of confidence, looking forward to seeing Chantal again, and to that happy life Galimard was so sure of.

We were all conscious that the summer holidays were coming to an end. I would have to get the children back to England for school, Chantal hers to Paris, and in her case she had also to start work in her firm. We were conscious also of the coming parting, and so were the children. They planned to write to each other, each in their respective languages, and correct each other in their replies.

I encouraged them. My parents, who had loved France, had encouraged me in taking up the teaching post in Figeac when I graduated all those years ago, my father firmly believing that to be really cultured, one should know another country as well as one's own, preferably France. He was a thoughtful, bookish man, and had encouraged me in my writing.

One day Chantal said to me, 'I'm going to take you to visit Simone and Jean. She was my nurse, then she married our gardener and they stayed on with my father until they were too old to work.'

'Am I being taken to see if they approve of me?' I said.

She laughed. 'I value their opinion. I should have taken it before I married François.'

We set off in my car, and as we drove past the church, she said, 'I should like us to be married there. Last time it was Paris, at my mother-in-law's insistence. I should have realized then that she was a very domineering woman, and that her son was like her, only more so. I'm sorry to say we had frequent quarrels, François and me. I was headstrong, he was like his mother. He didn't value my opinion, and we quarrelled a lot. A few years after our marriage, I noticed that he had begun to drink heavily, and if I mentioned it, he grew quite violent. I have the scar I showed you to prove it.'

You never told me how you got it,' I said, remembering. 'Was it really a skiing incident?'

'No, I can tell you now. François's behaviour became worse, as did his drinking. Had I been older and wiser, I would have realized he had something on his mind. A friend, to whom I confided my worries about his drinking, told me that he was mixed up with an undesirable group of people, and there were rumours going around about him. We were at the château for the weekend, and we had had a miserable trip down, quarrelling most of the time. This particular night he drank too much at dinner, and I was so annoyed at him that I told him that I knew he was involved in something . . . crooked?' She raised an eyebrow in query.

'Fishy?' I proposed.

'Feeshy, and that I knew he was keeping bad company, and that he was being watched. I'll never forget his face

119

when I said this. We were standing in the drawing room, and he staggered towards me, white-faced, eyes blazing, his hand raised, threateningly. I retreated, scared of him, and fell, cutting my forehead against the edge of an armoire. He helped me to my feet, full of apologies, indeed weeping, but I ran from the room into the kitchen where I knew I would find Simone. She wanted me to let Jean drive me to the hospital, but I wouldn't allow that because I didn't want anyone to know. Perhaps the cut should have been stitched, but in any case it healed quite soon, with Simone's help, and so no one knew except Simone and Jean and, of course, François. You are the first person I've told.'

'Was that when you got divorced?'

'No, you may not believe this, but I was sorry for him. He had been a handsome, proud man when I married him, but obviously weak, and he had fallen into bad company. He begged me to stay with him, and I thought I must support him because the cat would soon be out of the bag . . . first feesh and then cats!' We were in the car and she laughed. I saw she was weeping. 'I love those English expressions . . . that's why I'm marrying you,' she said, putting her head on my shoulder. She dabbed at her eyes with her handkerchief. 'I suppose I was thinking of the children and the disgrace to them. In the event it never came to anything, because his family stepped in, and everything was hushed up. I left him then, and joined up with my present firm.'

'Here was I thinking you were a hard woman,' I said, 'and you're as soft as butter underneath.'

'Soft as butter,' she repeated. 'I like it.'

When we arrived at our destination, she had quite recovered, and was first out of the car. It was an old cottage on the road past the church, stone-built, pantiled, with a *pigeonnier*, and although there was no garden at the front, I could see that there was a wide view of the *causse* at the back.

She had knocked, and I could see her talking to an elderly woman supporting herself with a stick. She beckoned to me and called, 'Come and meet Simone!'

I got out of the car and joined them at the open door. 'My

120

fiancé, Chantal said. 'Martin Woodbridge, Madame Simone Bertel.'

'*Enchanté*,' I said, shaking hands.

'Is this true, Madame?' the woman said. 'She is such a tease, Monsieur, that I never know whether to believe her or not.'

'Quite true,' I said, smiling.

'*Entrez*,' she said. 'I'm sorry, but my husband is in bed today. We both suffer from arthritis, but his bones were protesting louder than mine. This always happens when the summer is drawing to a close. But what about the tragedy in the village, Chantal?' She turned to her. 'Such a nice boy, that. I always said Marie would be the death of him.' We were now standing in the kitchen with its view over the *causse*, and when I exclaimed about it, she said, 'That's thanks to Chantal. She knew we wouldn't be happy away from the *causse*. Our room at the château had the same view.'

I had time to look at her while she was speaking. She was old, certainly, with grey hair in a bun, but her black eyes were bright and intelligent, and she moved pretty freely as she went about the kitchen, getting cups and saucers from a cupboard and biscuits from a tin.

'I'm sorry to hear your husband is indisposed,' I said.

'Ah, that's how it goes. Fortunately, I am fit and well and able to take care of him.' She shrugged. 'Enough about us. I hear you occupy Monsieur Maury's old cottage, Monsieur. You are English?'

'Yes,' I said. 'My wife and I came to Bernay and fell in love with it. But she died, and I met Chantal, and fortunately she has consented to marry me.'

'As long as she does not make the same mistake as the last time. What is your profession, Monsieur?'

'I'm a writer.'

'Well, that's harmless enough,' she said. I looked at Chantal and her eyes were dancing.

'This young lady is spirited, Monsieur. I speak as someone who has known her for a long time. You are taking on quite a lot.'

'Are you warning me off?' I said, laughing.

She pointed at me, smiling, and said to Chantal, 'He has a sense of humour, this one. He should do.'

'You give us your blessing, Simone?' Chantal said.

'Would it matter? Once you make up your mind nothing will change it. Have you asked Lenore and Mathius what they think?'

'It's their idea, Simone. Martin has two children about the same age, so we shall all be happy together.'

'When will the wedding take place?'

'We think next year some time at the church in Bernay. I want the whole village to be there, and you and Jean, Easter possibly, to include the children.'

'I hope it's Easter as I doubt if Jean and I can last till the summer.'

'We'll try for Easter. May I take Martin to see Jean, Simone?'

'You know you may. Come along.'

The man lying in bed looked pretty frail, but he tried to sit up when we came into the bedroom. 'Here's a surprise for you, Jean,' his wife said, propping him up with pillows. 'Chantal with her fiancé. He's called Martin.'

Chantal kissed him, and said, 'Are you pleased for me, Jean?'

'Are you pleased? That's the main thing.' He extended a hand to me. 'Martin. Welcome, and congratulations. We want her to be happy.'

'I'll be happy, Jean,' she said, 'and you must get well to come to our wedding at Easter.'

'It's just the medicine I needed. I'll get well. And are Mathius and Lenore pleased?'

'Very. Martin has two children also, Betsy and Nick, so already they are good friends. We're really marrying for their benefit.'

The man looked at me. 'That is Chantal. How can we tell if she is joking or not?'

'I think I can tell.'

'That is good.' He lay back on his pillows. Chantal kissed him.

'We'll go now, Jean. See you at Easter?'

I shook hands with him. 'She needs someone to look after her, that one,' he said to me. 'And now this happening in the village. I never approved of Marie. She caused a lot of trouble in the château while she was there. One couldn't believe anything she said. But Henri! From the time she appeared he was her willing slave.'

'He worries about this business, you know,' his wife said when she was showing us out. 'He never trusted Marie.'

'Martin will have a reply to that, Simone, one of his English sayings. Come on, darling.' She looked at me, smiling.

'It will all come out in the wash,' I said.

'It will all come out . . .' she repeated. 'Oh, yes, I see! Isn't he clever, Simone?'

We had another engagement that day. We were all meeting in the barn in the hope of seeing the owls flying. Mathius and Nick had seen them already, and they had arranged that the girls and Chantal and I should come to the barn at nine o'clock. They both had torches, and they asked us to sit on bales of hay which they had arranged. 'The stalls,' Nick said. We were commanded not to talk, and Chantal and I sat together, she with an arm round Lenore, I with an arm round Betsy. Our presence had alarmed the owls, and they were wheeling over our heads, their white faces ghostly in the torchlight. Martin showed us a photograph of the baby owls taken in spring, and when I looked at the four little monkey faces peering over the edge of the nest, I whispered to Chantal, 'Like our four?' She nodded and I hoped she was feeling as sentimental as I was, and very happy, a good happiness, mixed with certainty.

Betsy said, when we were home in the cottage, 'I don't know why, but I felt like crying tonight, watching those owls, and seeing that picture Mathius had of the babies. I was so happy.'

'I think we all were,' I said. 'Happy because we've met Mathius and Lenore and their mother, but not sad because it's been an important holiday, this.' And then, 'I want you to tell me truly, are you both happy that I'm marrying Chantal, and that Bernay will be your home for the next few years?'

Nick looked at Betsy. 'You first.'

'You probably don't realize, Daddy,' she said, 'that many of our school friends have been in the same position. Their parents separating, then a new parent. With us it's different. Mummy died, but we both realize we'll leave you in the future, and we want to feel that you'll be happy too.'

'We like Chantal,' Nick said. 'She'll be a good stepmother. We've talked it over with Mathius and Lenore, and they're quite happy with you too. So don't worry, Dad. We can think for ourselves, and we all think it's a jolly good idea.'

'I'm pleased about that,' I said. 'We'll probably get married in the church here at Easter, when the four of you are on holiday and you'll be able to come. It should be a great shindig.' I surprised myself. It wasn't a word I generally used. I must pass it on to Chantal.

We were sitting round the kitchen table. I stretched out my arms, and so did they. Our fingers touched, and we were happy. It had been a good day.

'Tomorrow's the fête in the village,' I said. 'It will be a good end to the holiday. Chantal will expect us to turn up.'

'Try and stop us,' Betsy said.

'Yes, try,' Nick said. I thought his eyes were wet. I saw my father in him.

Seventeen

The children were excited on the day of the fête. There were numerous telephone calls between them and Mathius and Lenore about arrangements. Mathius had been appointed as one of the organizers. This was his first year, and he was taking his duties very seriously. I felt sad that I shouldn't see Chantal for some time, but we had promised each other to perhaps meet in London or Paris for a weekend before Easter. She would take care of the arrangements with Monsieur Vincennes, the priest in Bernay. I had already spoken to him, and signed the necessary forms.

I drove up to the château with Betsy and Nick and picked up Chantal, Mathius and Lenore. The children piled into the back, and Chantal came in beside me.

'Hello!' she said, and kissed my cheek.

It was eight o'clock. The village was lit by the setting sun, and there were quite a lot of the village children scurrying about the field where the fête was being held. It was at the top of the village, and the view was the same as from Simone and Jean's cottage, as if on top of the world. It was a delectable village, I thought, cosying round the *place* but having this lovely viewpoint where one could stretch one's eyes. I felt I belonged. 'I love Bernay,' I said to Chantal, and she smiled at me. 'I love you,' her eyes said.

We parked, aided by Mathius, who was taking his duties very seriously, and followed behind him to the fairground

Already a helter-skelter had been set up, a tall tower which one slid round on a carpet, Mathius told me, as well as a merry-go-round with fearsome horses with painted nostrils, and numerous stalls. The mayor welcomed us as we reached the gate, and I was introduced to him by Chantal.

'Good luck, Mathius,' Chantal said to him, and I added, 'Go to it!' He was to cut the ribbon across the opening into the field and declare the fête open.

'He's quite nervous,' Chantal said to me as we stood back with the girls. 'He's been rehearsing.'

'He'll rise to the occasion,' I said, remembering that was one of my father's favourite sayings if I had to face any challenge.

The mayor made a short speech introducing Mathius and praising his grandfather, the Count, and what he had done for the village, and then presented a pair of scissors to Mathius. Lenore gave him a sisterly push.

He strode up to the ribbon which had taken the place of the gate, looked around, and said, in a loud voice, 'I declare the fête open. Good luck to everyone. I hope you all win something at the stalls.' He then cut the ribbon with a flourish. Everyone cheered, and I looked at Chantal. Her eyes were bright and fixed on her son. I squeezed her arm, and the mayor shouted, 'Three cheers for Mathius!'

Everyone then trooped through the open gate, and Mathius joined us with that look on his face that all young boys wear when they have been asked to take on the burdens of maturity. 'Well done, Mathius.' His mother kissed him, and we all surrounded him, the girls kissing his cheeks.

He shook them off. 'Come on!' he said to Nick, and they set off, the girls trailing behind.

'That's his first ordeal,' I said to Chantal. 'He did very well.'

'They're so sweet,' she said, and I knew what she meant.

We followed in their footsteps and found them at the shooting gallery. Even Betsy and Lenore were having a go, and Chantal said to me, 'Show them how it's done!'

My efforts were dismal, and I thought their father could have probably done much better. 'Writers are too peaceful a breed,' I said, 'to excel in sport.'

I joined in the three-legged race with Nick, and thanks to him we came in first, and were awarded with a fluffy teddy bear coloured pink, which we presented to Chantal.

We left the children after a time and walked about, greeting villagers and other people she knew who had come from the surrounding countryside. I was introduced to many of them, and basked in the aura of being presented as Chantal's affianced.

It grew dark, and the lights were switched on. We could hear music coming from a corner of the field. We walked over, and saw that a platform had been erected there. Quite a lot of people were dancing on it to a vigorous polka. 'That seems to be the favourite dance around here,' Chantal said.

'Would you like to join in?' I asked her.

'Let's wait until they play a waltz,' she said. 'It suits us better.'

We stood watching until the band changed its tempo to the Blue Danube. 'May I have the pleasure?' I said.

We joined the dancers, and I intercepted some curious looks as people danced past us. Chantal had an arm round my neck, and was whispering in my ear. 'Don't worry. They're all interested in us. I don't think François was as popular as you.'

We floated around in a blissful state, and I thought, is this me, in a French village, engaged to the daughter of the château? How my life had changed!

I was rudely awakened from this pleasant state when I felt a tap on my shoulder. It was Pierre, the painter, who had worked for me in the cottage. 'Excuse me,' he said, and taking Chantal in his arms, danced away with her. I retreated to the side of the floor, and watched my love being whirled expertly by Pierre, whom I quickly realized was a performer and had chosen Chantal as a suitable partner. As they whirled past me, Chantal threw a glance at me, her eyes dancing, and I knew she knew what I was thinking. How wonderful, I thought.

I also thought the correct response for me was to choose a partner and see what I could do. I looked around. Wasn't that the butcher's wife, Madame Vigny, I thought, spying a woman with yellow hair done up on top of her head, and wearing a poppy-strewn dress? I had first noticed her when I went to their shop to buy lamb chops because of the immaculate whiteness of the coat she wore, never a stain on it, her yellow hair done up in elaborate whirls. How was it, I had thought, that her husband, who wore a striped blue apron, showed signs of having had to deal with beasts in their abattoir state, whereas Madame's turnout was flawless and wouldn't have disgraced a *salon de thé*. Perhaps she stuck to easily-handled articles like sausages and pâté and chops, while he dealt with messy liver and minced beef.

I strode over to where Madame was sitting with some other ladies of the village. 'May I have the pleasure?' I said, bowing.

Her face showed surprise which quickly melted into gratification as she rose to her feet, casting a swift triumphant glance at her companions.

We sailed away. 'Good band,' I said, heaving her considerable bulk around. I thought longingly of Chantal's slim figure.

'*Oui*, M'sieur.' I had noticed in her shop that her small canary-like voice didn't match her appearance.

'They come from Souillac, I see.' I nodded at the band. I had noticed printed on the drum, the words, 'The Souillac Five.'

'*Oui*, M'sieur.'

Was she terrified of me? Would she be more at ease if I asked her what her sausages were like these days?'

We were dancing in silence while I racked my brains for some kind of chit-chat, when, to my immense relief, the mayor tapped my shoulder. He was equal to her in bulk. They should make a good pair, I thought, as I relinquished my partner gladly.

I retired to the edge of the floor again, and watched Chantal being whirled around by different partners. Her full-skirted white dress swung out as she was spun, it seemed, by the entire village. Occasionally she threw me a mischievous glance, rolling her eyes, and I responded with a tight-lipped smile.

Guy Rosier joined me where I was standing. His face was stern. 'I've just been talking to the policeman from Souillac. He generally looks in. He tells me that Marie Leroy has committed suicide! Difficult to believe, isn't it?'

128

'Terrible news if it's true.' I was surprised, to put it mildly. 'Madame Gibert ought to know. Have you any details?'

'Just that her mother found her dead in bed. The baby was crying. That alerted her.'

'Thibaud,' I said. I don't know why I said his name, but I saw him suddenly on his royal tour in his mother's arms at the hotel.

I looked around the room. Chantal was dancing with the butcher. Tit for tat, I thought. I strode over and tapped him on the shoulder. 'Excuse me,' I said.

'Thank God you rescued me,' Chantal said as we danced away. 'He smells of blood.' 'Fee fi fo fum' occurred to me, but it wasn't the time to say it.

'I have bad news for you. Let's go and find the children.'

'Tell me,' she said when we had left the dancing and were walking towards the stalls.

'Now I can't vouch for this, but it comes from the policeman from Souillac, via Guy Rosier. He says that Marie Leroy has committed suicide!'

'No!' She turned towards me. 'And the baby?'

'No, he's still alive.'

'That Thibaud is a survivor,' she said. 'For the moment I'm just going to tell the children that I've had bad news, and I have to use the telephone. We'll go back to your house or mine, and return and collect them later. They won't want to come away just yet.'

'Are you going to phone Galimard?'

'Yes, I think I can ask him.'

'Perhaps he has already tried to phone you?'

'Perhaps. Let's go to your house. It's nearer, and it will save me disturbing the Vilars.'

'I think that would be better.'

I parked the car in front of the cottage, and unlocking the door, led Chantal into the sitting room. 'I have his number here,' I said, lifting my address book.

I gave it to her, and poured out two glasses of wine, put one in front of her and sat down beside her. 'Go ahead,' I said.

Fortunately, he was in. I listened to the one-sided

conversation. 'Please forgive me for phoning you at meal-time. I've just heard disturbing news at the fête, presumably from a Souillac policeman.' Pause. I saw her face change, become serious. There was a long pause while she listened. 'Dreadful!' Shorter pause. 'That's good of you.' Pause. 'I understand. I leave for Paris tomorrow, but you can get me there at my flat, or work-place. I shall be happy to assist you. Terrible! Yes, there's the baby.' Another shorter pause. 'Thank you. Goodbye.'

'Yes, it's true.' She turned to me. 'She left a letter. It will be used at the trial, which is coming off in February at Cahors. I may try to come back for it. I'll see. But he'll verify the news and let me know.'

I thought, this is her affair, I'm only an onlooker, but it didn't prevent me voicing my thoughts. 'If the letter she left contradicts what she told me, I wonder how it will affect Henri at his trial. And there's the added factor of the baby. I don't expect his mother-in-law will want to take care of him. I've a feeling that this is going to change everything.'

'Who knows? I'm so sad for them, Marie gone, Henri in prison. There's no point in speculating till we know what was in her letter. And it may not be possible for Pierre Galimard to divulge it to me.'

'Would you call it a *crime passionnel* now, Chantal?'

'It's not clear-cut from a legal point of view until we know what's in the letter. I see life, Martin, you write about it. You can't write the story until you have worked out the developments, or in this case, know the contents of the letter.'

'Don't let's discuss it any more,' I said. 'Now that we're here, and we're going to say goodbye soon. Would you like to come upstairs with me and say goodbye properly?'

'Is that what would happen in your novel?' She teased me, smiling.

'Definitely.'

We were so engrossed that we forgot to pick up the children. Fortunately we heard the band marching down the street, playing. 'That's the end of the fête,' Chantal said, sitting up in bed. She put her hand to her mouth. 'The children! We said we would pick them up!' We assembled ourselves and dashed downstairs and I opened the door. The procession was marching past us. We watched as the big drum came into view, the drummer banging away, the people walking behind it, chatting, laughing, waving. 'The Grand Procession,' Chantal said, '*de rigeur.*' Then we saw Betsy and Nick, Mathius and Lenore marching along. 'Here they come,' she said, turning to me, abashed.

'Don't blame me,' I said, putting an arm round her shoulders.

The children wheeled in as they came to our open door, still marching. 'You forgot to come for us,' they chorused.

'Into the kitchen!' I shouted, like a commander, and Chantal and I followed them. We were helpless with laughter when we all collapsed into chairs.

Betsy said, spluttering, 'We got tired waiting for you so we joined in behind the procession.'

'And there you were at the open door, ready to greet us.'

'I liked how we all wheeled in,' Mathius said.

'And how we were marching in time to the music,' Nick added.

'Was it bad news, *Maman*?' Mathius asked.

'It was to do with the Leroy case. I had to phone the detective dealing with it. I'll tell you more later.'

'OK.'

'How about some hot cocoa after all the excitement?' I asked. I admired how Chantal dealt with Mathius's enquiry.

Everyone was enthusiastic and lent a hand. When we were sitting round the table, I said, 'We'll be leaving early tomorrow. How about you, Chantal?'

'I've given up trying to beat the traffic. I'll have things to do at the château, so I aim to leave around twelve.'

'We'll make this a goodbye feast, then. It's sad, isn't it?'

'When shall we meet again?' Lenore appealed to her mother.

'Let's make plans. Martin and I will be in touch by telephone, and he may visit us in Paris. Isn't that right?' She looked at me.

'Yes, I'll get on with some work and then you can tell me when it's convenient.'

'It might be possible for Lenore and Mathius to visit us in England?'

'*Bonne idée*,' Mathius said.

'If it fits in with your visit?'

'Yes.'

'We'll see. And I think I may be at the château during the first part of the year,' Chantal said. 'I'd like to look in at the Leroy trial. You might be able to join me then, Martin.'

'We'll see. It's all looking very exciting. For all of us.'

I looked around the smiling faces. My family! 'My mind is buzzing with ideas,' I said to Chantal. 'In between, you and I have to get some work done, but, yes, we'll be able to work things out, and then we've got the long summer holidays ahead.'

Lenore said, 'I've just been thinking how complicated it is for you and Martin, *Maman,* with four of us to consider.' There were murmurs from the other three in agreement.

'It is not at all complicated, *cherie.* Martin and I have a ready-made family, and it makes it all the more exciting, *n'est-ce pas*, Martin?'

'It's wonderful for me, and for Betsy and Nick,' I said.

'Do you think we'll quarrel?' Betsy asked.

'*Naturellement*,' Chantal said. 'I'm looking forward to some good shindigs, that is a word Martin has taught me.'

'I don't remember,' I said. 'But I'm sure it's going to be fun.'

Saying goodbye was hard. We weren't going to meet in the morning, so this was it. I kissed Lenore, and hugged Mathius – I don't think he liked that – and while the children were busy saying their goodbyes, I hugged Chantal and we kissed.

The three of us stood at the open door of the cottage, waving to the three retreating figures going up the drive.

When I finally shut the door, Betsy went rushing up the stairs, and Nick said to me, his voice gruff, 'She'll be all right. She's always like that.'

The two of us washed up the cocoa cups and made the kitchen shipshape, and went upstairs together.

Eighteen

We had plenty to talk about on our way back to England, but once we got home, it was full speed ahead. There was a woman in the village whom Merle had employed for sewing, and I asked her if she could take over the task of sorting out the children's school trunks, sewing labels, packing and so on. This relieved me of that duty, and I was able to get into my study and open the letters that had accumulated during our absence. There was a surprise for me from my agent. She had sold my book on Agnès Sorel to a French publisher, who could arrange to have it translated for me if I wished. The terms were very good, and I was delighted with the sale. It had already earned me quite a lot of money, but I didn't think I would take on the translation. It was too time-consuming.

I would think about that, but as well, the publishers would like to lay on a publicity tour for me in France. I had a few delicious decisions to make, but it looked as if I might be visiting Paris fairly soon.

I telephoned Chantal with my news, and she was delighted, saying that she would look forward to an early visit from me. She hadn't heard from Pierre Galimard, but she had definitely decided to sit in on the trial at Cahors when it came off.

Betsy, Nick and I had a few treats before I drove them back to school, which was to me a melancholy business, although children seem to accept it fairly well. I suppose they were looking forward to meeting their friends again. I determined to take up my old life, and after I got home I made two or three trips to London to see friends, and also to tell them about Chantal. Their reactions varied, but in imparting information, it's better to be quite sure of your own decision. Most of them made remarks such as, 'Well, Martin, you could have knocked me over with a feather!' All were impressed when I told them that Chantal was a lawyer, and that she owned the château in the village where I had spent my holidays. The ruder ones said, 'Well, you've landed on your feet and no mistake.' The women were mostly interested in the four children we had between us, and either looked delighted for me, or doubtful. But I was not in a state to be easily influenced. I was very happy, and my frequent conversations with Chantal on the telephone only helped to increase my happiness.

I settled into my housewifely routine, tidying, taking linen to the laundry, cooking, gardening and managing about six hours of writing every day. There would be Easter and the wedding, but before that, I would be going to Paris, I hoped. The appointment with the publishers there came through, February the twenty-third, and I worked towards that date, enjoying my new life of anticipation.

I saw Margot every week for lunch, and when I broke the news about Chantal, to my surprise she seemed pleased. 'I never expected you not to marry again, Martin. From what you tell me, it sounds very satisfactory for the children.'

'Perhaps you would think of coming to our wedding at Easter,' I said. 'You could come with the children and myself when we leave for France.'

'Are you sure?' she said, looking pleased.

'Certainly. We're a bit short of Grannies on Chantal's side, and mine, of course, since my mother died, and I know she would like to meet you. You would find her very charming.'

I could see she was impressed with what I had told her about Chantal. 'She sounds very different from Merle, but I would be happy to meet her. Thank you, Martin.' For some reason we seemed to be getting on well together. Had I changed too?

With grief one goes through a series of changes, from despair to acceptance, and also through the feeling that one will never be really happy again. But I had been lucky, I had met Chantal, and the fact that she had understood how I felt also helped me through the ridiculous feeling that I was betraying Merle by feeling so happy.

When I left for Paris I felt I was setting out on a new journey, a new life. The fact that it bore no relation to my previous one helped in what they call 'the healing process', and when my taxi dropped me at Chantal's apartment block in Le Marais, I felt a wonderful sense of hope and security. I pressed the intercom at the side of an impressive wooden door. 'This is Martin,' I said.

'Hello. Come up, Martin.' Her voice in my ears made me feel I was twenty, instead of forty. I bounded up the wide staircase, passing the lift.

She was at the open door, looking lovely. The sight of her was enough to reassure me that I had chosen the right course. She held out her arms, and kissing her I said, 'It was too long.'

'But all the better for waiting.'

She led me into a huge room, full of light.

'This is lovely,' I said. We were standing at the windows which gave on to the green expanse of the Place de Vosges.

'You like it? I sold the family home, and the money I got was almost swallowed up in this.'

'And you look lovely too. Will the children be coming in soon?'

'No, they are staying over with schoolfriends. So we are alone for tonight. Does that suit you?'

'It suits me,' I said. 'I thought I'd fly back tomorrow evening after my interview with the publishers, since you are busy with court cases. And my plan about taking Mathius and Lenore back with me is no good now. Would you like me to take you out to dinner?'

'No, thank you. Some other time. But we have a lot of talking to do, and we are more private here. I have the table set in my kitchen.'

'Great! I've been thinking a lot about the Leroys. Have you anything to tell me?'

'Yes, I have. But first, we must eat. Come with me, Martin.'

I followed her into a gleaming kitchen, where I was given the task of opening bottles, while Chantal prepared a salad, which seemed to be a glorious concoction of herbs, Parma ham, vegetables I didn't recognize and the usual leaves. She had made a chocolate soufflé, which she showed me, saying, 'Did you know chocolate is the food of love?'

'So are these oysters,' I said, pointing to some in a bowl. She laughed at me.

'I don't think we need them, do you?'

'We have a saying, "Absence makes the heart grow fonder",' I said.

When we sat down to dinner, Chantal said, 'I have to tell you that Galimard couldn't divulge to me the exact contents of Marie Leroy's letter. He apologizes, but says the gist of it is that Marie and Henri had a quarrel, and she got so angry with him and Baron both that she took the gun and went and shot her lover. She says Henri tried to stop her. To prove her statement the gun would have to be found to obtain finger-prints, but although they have searched around the mill and even in the river, they have been unable to find it. I shall go to the trial, of course, and let you know the outcome, but in the meantime, the solution lies in the finding of the gun.'

'Does he persist in saying he did it?'

'Yes, he sticks to his story. He has all the stubbornness of a weak man.'

'Or a man who wants to protect his wife.'

'You are a romantic, *cheri*, and I love you for it. Meantime, tell me your plans for tomorrow.'

'I shall take the Metro from the Bastille, and see my publisher, my appointment is at eleven in the morning. I've booked an evening flight back to London, since you'll be busy. You told me that on the phone, and I don't want to get in your hair.'

'Get in my hair? Entangled with me?'

'*C'est ça.* But if you like, I could take you out to lunch in Paris?'

'I wish I could say, yes. But *ce n'est pas possible.* I shall be in court all day.'

'I'm getting used to you not always being available, but you did say you'd give up work when you were forty, so meantime I shall have to work doubly hard to pass the time.'

'Do not worry. It's exciting, don't you find?' It wasn't possible to be in Chantal's company and not laugh most of the time. Her sense of humour ran through everything she said.

When we were having coffee in her sitting room, she put out the overhead lights, and we sat together on the sofa with only a soft light on the table beside us. We became sentimental, talking of the wedding plans and our life together, and the children, and how exciting it would be to watch their careers develop, and picturing ourselves, still together, still happy with each other.

In bed, we went on talking, propped up on the pillows. There was so much to say, but little time to say it. We grew tired, and lay down, confessing to each other that we had been deliberately delaying doing so because the prospect was so exciting. Chantal said it was the chocolate which was the aphrodisiac, but I was convinced it was the oysters, but agreed later that we hadn't needed any stimulants.

We went to sleep in each other's arms, but although I was tired, I woke at three o'clock, disturbed by memories of the Leroys, because of what Chantal had told me. I remembered the time Henri had taken us to the mill, and being in the boat with him, rowing towards his fishing place. And that stone wall which had been covered with the small blue butterflies of the *causse*, and how he had rapidly scaled it. I saw the wall clearly, rough limestone, devoid of butterflies, and how I had wondered if there were any hidden foot-holes for him. His 'party piece', he had called it. There had been clumps of greenery growing out of spaces between the stones, especially near the top where I had seen his hand grip. Could it have served as a hiding place? For the rifle? I lay, seeing Henri flat against the wall, his left hand outstretched, feeling for the space between the stones. I knew with certainty what I had to do. I propped myself on my elbow and looked down at Chantal. She was sleeping quietly, her dark eyelashes lying on her cheeks, and her mouth curved in a half-smile. I would tell her about that time we had gone fishing with Henri, and how he had demonstrated to us his skill at scaling the wall where we had tied up the boat, and that I had to get in touch with Galimard. She would have his telephone number. I was convinced as I lay down that what I remembered was important.

I got up before eight, went to the kitchen and made some coffee, found cups, and put them on a tray, carried it into the bedroom. I put the tray on the bedside table, then gently shook Chantal's shoulder. 'Come on, sleepy-head, you'll be late for work,' I said. Her dark hair lay over her bare shoulder.

She opened her eyes. 'It's you, Martin.' She held out her arms, and I bent to kiss her.

'Who did you think it was? I had to waken you to tell you about a sudden memory I had,' I said. 'It's very important. I've brought you some coffee.'

'Oh, how clever of you! I don't begin to operate until I have my morning coffee.' She yawned, patting her mouth. 'Did you sleep well, my darling?'

'Except for thinking about the Leroys. I think I know where Henri hid the gun.' I described the fishing trip with Henri. 'It may be prescience on my part,' I said, 'but I'm convinced that the gun will be found tucked into that wall. Don't you think I should phone Galimard?'

She had sipped her coffee while I was speaking. 'Now, I'm functioning. It's incredible, but I too am convinced you've solved the mystery. Yes, I do think you should phone Pierre. What time is it?'

'Eight thirty.'

'Eight thirty. I must catch the Metro at nine thirty to be at the court for ten.' She flung back the bedclothes and got quickly out of bed. 'I'll have a shower while you telephone. It's a good time. He won't have left the house yet, especially since his wife is pregnant. He will help her before he leaves home, like a good husband. On you go, Martin, then you can have a shower and we'll both go on the Metro together. You'll find his home number in the red book beside the telephone.'

Certainly Galimard's voice was sleepy, unlike his usual brisk way of speaking. He listened to me without interrupting until I had finished. 'This is bizarre, Monsieur,' he said, 'but some of *my* best thinking is done in bed! I'm inclined to believe that the place you tell me of could well be the hiding place for the rifle. Where no one would think to look. I'll get on to Souillac and have them go to the place you have described. Let's hope they have a policeman who can scale walls!'

'That might not be necessary,' I said. 'The ledge was near the top. There might be a path above it.'

'You could be right. They'll have to work it out for themselves.'

'I'm in Paris. Could you telephone Madame Gibert and tell her of the outcome, and she will let me know.'

'Certainly. I'm just as keen to know as you. I'll probably go with them. Thank you very much, Monsieur. You may have done the police a great service. I'll get in touch with them right away.'

I had been going to ask how his wife was, but he had hung up.

Chantal was in legal gear and looking very fetching, black suit, white blouse, and hair pulled back. I told her Galimard was going to act right away.

'Good,' she said. 'They can't afford to ignore what you've remembered. Now you go and have your shower. We just have time to have breakfast before we go for the Metro.' She kissed me, saying, 'That's a reward for being clever, or clairvoyant, whatever it is. I didn't realize you had this gift!'

'All writers have it,' I said. 'We would be very useful in court.'

We set off for the Bastille Metro, and parted at the Court. We had said our goodbyes in the apartment, so it was only a brief embrace, After all she was an *avocat*.

My interview with the publishers was satisfactory. They seemed to hold out a great future for the book. They had plans for signings in Paris book shops, and a visit to Loches where Agnès Sorel had spent most of her life. I walked around Montmartre to pass the time before my plane, had lunch in a café there, and wondered how I had ever had the nerve to have my portrait done in the *place* by one of the artists who frequented it, as I had done in my youth. Sheer flattery, I supposed, then went to the collecting place for the bus to take me to the airport. I felt satisfied with my visit to Paris, and was weary when I got back to Kent. I fell into bed, missing Chantal, and realising that it would be no ordinary marriage, this. It would have to be worked at, but it would all be worthwhile.

Nineteen

Easter and the wedding were rushing towards us. The next time I met Chantal, she had spent the day in the court, where Marie's suicide note had been read out. 'I have a copy of it here. Would you like to read it?' she said. We were in her sitting room in Le Marais.

'No, thank you,' I said. 'You're marrying a tender-hearted man. You read it out to me.'

She went to her desk, and came back with a piece of paper in her hand. 'I'm supposed to have a heart of steel?'

'You're an *avocat*.'

'All right. I promise you, it's heartbreaking.' She began to read:

> I have decided to take my life because of the mess I've made of it, I, Marie Leroy.
>
> Henri and I had lots of quarrels about Raymond Baron and the baby. One night in the midst of one of them, he said, 'I would kill that man if I could get my hands on him.' I said, 'All right. I happen to know he's waiting at the old mill house for me. He's going to take us away, Thibaud and me. If you want him dead, now is your chance!'
>
> I was so angry I ran and fetched his rifle and pushed it at him, shouting, 'Kill him if you love me so much! Aren't you my husband? You want me back so much, you go and kill him!' But true to type he just stared at me and said, 'You're crazy, you need to stop this.' Fierce Henri, hunter of wild boars!
>
> I was mad with Henri but I knew Raymond wouldn't take me away. He promised and promised

141

but it was all just words. I knew he was waiting for me at the mill. I took the gun and walked out of the room, went to where Thibaud was sleeping, stowed the gun beside him in his carry-cot, and took it out to the car. I strapped Thibaud in, and drove to meet Raymond. As I was driving on to the road I saw Henri in the rear mirror chasing after the car and waving at me, trying to get me to stop, but I paid no attention. I had the gun which Henri had taught me to use for protection.

When I parked the car beside the mill house, I had one idea in mind. I crept to the broken window of the room where Raymond was. I saw he was bent over his rucksack, packing it, and when I called he looked up. I think I shot him between the eyes. This is the truth. I told an Englishman who had stayed at the hotel that Henri had done it, but this was not true. I told him the story the way I wished it had happened.

I came back to the car, my heart broken. Thibaud was still sleeping. I sat there for a long time, knowing that I had shot my lover in a fit of madness. I was sitting there when Henri appeared. He was on a bicycle that he must have borrowed from one of the hotel guests. He said, 'Marie, come home, you have to stop this before you do something you can't undo.'

I thrust the rifle at Henri and said, 'It's too late. Here! I've done it for you. Now, you get rid of this.'

Henri looked at me in horror. 'You've murdered a man!'

'You didn't love me enough to do it for me,' I said. 'If you love me at all, you'll get rid of this gun, but if you turn me in, I'll know you didn't love me any more than Raymond did.' I knew the tears were running down my face. Henri looked at me for a long time before he took the gun from me, then went away quietly.

While he was gone I lifted the baby over and tried to quieten him. The noise of our voices had frightened him, I think. He was crying so hard that you would have thought he knew that I had killed his father. When I lifted my head from comforting him, I saw Henri standing outside the car. He raised his hands to show me that they were empty. I know he stood there for a long time, looking at us. Then he was gone.

So you see I don't deserve to live. Raymond deserved to die. He kept promising me that he would look after me and the baby. But I loved him.

My mother is ashamed of me. Last night she told me I would have to leave her house because the neighbours were talking about me. I don't know where to go. I can't see . . . the room is getting dark and fading away . . . the doctor gave me pills to help me to sleep, and I've swallowed a lot of them. Thibaud is crying. I daren't lift him in my arms . . .

If Henri is released for my sake, he might take care of Thibaud. He grew quite fond of him although he was not his baby. Thibaud is crying. I killed his father. Please release Henri so that he can look after him.

God forgive me. I killed Raymond, my lover.

Chantal raised her face to me. Tears were running down her face. 'It's so sad,' she said.

I got up and put my arms round her. 'Here,' I said, 'you're not supposed to cry. I'm the tender-hearted one.'

'I know. But I knew them.'

'Yes,' I said. 'It's tragic. The power of love and jealousy. Now tell me the rest. What about the rifle?' She was sitting on the sofa and I sat down beside her, my arm round her shoulders.

'They found her fingerprints around the trigger. Her lawyer said that fortunately a member of the public, a former guest at the hotel, had been on a fishing expedition with Henri, and he remembered Henri's prowess at scaling an old wall. He suggested that Henri might have scaled the same wall on the night of the murder and hidden the rifle in a crevice. This proved to be the case. We are indebted to this man for his suggestion.'

'Good.' I was pleased that my name hadn't been mentioned, not pleased with my part in this tragedy, but I had done the right thing, I knew.

'So what was the result?' I asked.

'Not guilty. There was the confessional letter from Marie who was deemed to be of sound mind, and because of the long time he had been held in custody, he was immediately released. The prosecution wanted to charge him with concealing evidence, but in the end they took into account the fact that he tried to stop her and that he had a child to support, and they let him go. The judge said it was a tragic case, and he hoped Henri would find consolation in looking after Thibaud, the baby.'

'Thibaud triumphs,' I said.

'Yes, a trouper. I spoke to Henri after the trial. He was a shadow of his former self. But he had made plans. He intended to go to Normandy and buy a hotel with the proceeds from Le Tilleul, and take Thibaud with him.'

'Good luck to him,' I said.

'The hotel at Bernay has been sold to a local couple, you may remember them, the butcher and his wife, Monsieur and Madame Vigny, and they intended to improve it.'

I groaned. 'I hope they don't spoil it,' I said. 'They'll put a pool in, and their clientele will become very different. The hunters won't come, and the village people might stop dropping in for a glass of wine.'

'Don't let your imagination run away with you,' Chantal said to me. 'Do you know what I think? Henri will marry a nice buxom Normandy girl who will become a good mother to Thibaud, and when Thibaud grows up he'll come back and buy the hotel which will be up for sale because the Vignys have become too old to run it, and he'll change it again. That will be in the twenty-first century, so who's to say what it will be like?'

'What a fertile imagination you have!' I laughed.

'Are you jealous?'

'Not at all. But I'm amazed. I thought your legal brain wouldn't allow you to speculate.'

'Oh, there are surprises in store for you,' she said. 'When I retire I might even become a writer.'

'No,' I said. 'That's my patch.'

Came the day when the children, Margot and I were travelling to Bernay for the wedding. Numerous cases were stored in the boot, with all the wedding clothes. Margot sat with me in the front, and Betsy and Nick were in the back. I felt acutely nervous, but driving through France seemed to calm me, and the thought of seeing Chantal again made me feel very happy. I had bought a ring for her, a band of gold with a circlet of diamonds set round a sapphire, which I hoped to slip on her finger at the ceremony.

We arrived tired. At least, that applied to Margot and me, but the children were excited and happy to meet Lenore and Mathius again. Chantal made Margot feel very welcome, I could see, and she was led away to be shown her room, after she had been given the requisite cup of tea to revive her. When Chantal came down again she was smiling. 'What a sweet old lady,' she said. And to Betsy and Nick, 'How do you address her?'

'Grannie,' they said.

'Well, Mathius and Lenore will say the same. She must be made to feel welcome.'

'Are you sure we should stay at the château?' I asked.

'Why not?'

'You and I are supposed not to meet before the ceremony. It's considered unlucky.'

'But that is for a young bride and bridegroom. You and I have had enough bad luck. No, I have engaged cars. We will all leave together for the church.'

I gave in, glad to do so. Neither of us cared much for protocol, and we had to think of the children. They were happier here.

Chantal and I had been very busy. Chantal had to clear up some work before Easter, and so had I. My cottage in Kent had to be made tidy, and arrangements made with a handyman in the village to look after the garden. Margot had been kind enough to go with Betsy to buy a dress for the wedding, and I had promised her that Margot would allow her to exercise her own taste. 'Chantal wants me in pink, that's bad enough, but Grannie will try to put me into frills!'

Nick and I had new suits made. Because of him being the youngest, Chantal had said that Nick, Mathius and myself were to be in ordinary lounge suits like him, so that he wouldn't feel out of place. 'Anyhow,' she said, 'they're more suitable for a country wedding.' Her dress was a secret, but she would like the children to walk behind us in pairs. No bridesmaids or best man.

Madame Vilar had prepared rooms for us, and after a swim to freshen us up, we had an early dinner and went off to bed. To spare the Vilars' sensitivities, Chantal and I didn't sleep together. Betsy shared with Lenore, and Nick with Mathius.

In the morning we had breakfast and assembled in the drawing room, waiting for the cars to arrive. Chantal looked entrancing in a white dress and large-brimmed hat, also in white. Lenore and Betsy were both in pink, at her request, and the boys and I were in sober sub-fusc. 'As long as you don't have to wear pink bow ties,' Betsy had said. Monsieur Vilar had provided white carnations for our buttonholes and a bouquet of white lilies for Chantal. The girls had been in the garden and had made themselves wreaths of white marguerites to wear in their hair. Grannie Strong, this was how Chantal addressed her, was in grey lace. I thought we made a very presentable wedding party.

When we drove through the village, there were a few people at their gates, waving, but when we got to the church, it seemed the whole village was there. They trooped in after us as we went in.

The ceremony went off quite well, but the only part of it that stayed in my mind was the feeling of deep satisfaction I got when I slipped the ring on Chantal's finger, and our eyes met. Hers were wet, but she smiled at me, and that was enough.

She had arranged a lunch at the hotel for us and all the village, and Monsieur and Madame Vigny, did us proud. I wondered if any butcher and his wife in England could have prepared such a meal. There were aperitifs at the beginning to toast Chantal and I, and on tap, it seemed.

We started off with *Salade aux gésiers,* washed down with plenty of the rich Cahors wine, rich enough to make all the villagers look quite bucolic, I thought, or maybe it was that the whole affair for me was bathed in a rosy glow. Then *saumon fumé*, served with white Bergerac, then *Confit de Canard,* with the delicious Cahors again.

At this stage Chantal and I were pleasantly merry, and we raised our glasses to Monsieur and Madame Vigny, who, in her crinoline dress of white, trimmed with pink, showing her plump shoulders, almost outdid my bride.

But I haven't finished yet. There were all the delicious cheeses of the region, and profiteroles in a cone shape that Chantal told me were traditional at a French wedding.

We had speeches. I welcomed everyone there, and paid a heartfelt tribute to my beautiful bride. I congratulated the Vignys on the wedding feast, and said that if I had had any doubts of coming to live in Bernay, that had convinced me.

Chantal replied, praising my attributes ridiculously, and England, for producing someone like me, and hoping I would be welcomed by everyone in the village. 'He is really very nice,' she said, 'although he is English.'

The mayor raised his glass and asked everyone to do the same. 'To the Bernay family,' he said, 'and we welcome its new addition, Monsieur Martin Woodbridge, and his two children.'

Then Monsieur Vigny asked for a toast to be drunk to the happy couple. 'M'sieu Woodbridge has made himself one of us,' he said. There were cheers, at this stage, as I stood up to reply, deeply embarrassed.

I don't know what I said, I was drunk with happiness and good French wine. But when I looked at Chantal, her smiling face raised to me, I surprised myself, and possibly the guests by my lavish praise of her beauty and her brains.

But catching sight of the four children, sitting together, their smiling faces raised to us, I only managed to say something like, 'But as well as Chantal and Bernay accepting me, I have to mention our four children here today who have been instrumental in us coming together. My sincere thanks to them, and everyone here.'

The last one to speak was Monsieur Vincennes, the priest. He looked round the dining room and the happy faces raised to him. He held up his hand, as if in blessing.

'I'm sure,' he said, 'we'll never see a happier couple, and we rejoice in their happiness. I hesitate to introduce a serious note, but I feel it might be expected of me, and it is Chantal's wish that I bring it up. Recently we had a tragedy in the village, resulting in Henri Leroy being apprehended. But you will all be happy to know he will be released very soon. Marie committed suicide, and left a note taking the blame.'

Everyone went quiet. He went on: 'We should remember them as a young couple who ran the hotel with great expertise. I have seen him, and it is his intention to buy a hotel in Normandy and rear Thibaud there, whom you will all remember as a lovely child. Do not blame them, do not be bitter in your thoughts about them, think of Henri Leroy trying to make a new life for himself in Normandy, and admire him for taking the little child into his care. There is a lesson for us all there.' He sat down.

There was silence for a few minutes, then Mathius stood up.

'This is a wedding,' he said. 'Let's dance!' He waved to the Souillac Five, who else, and shouted, 'Take it away!' – to the manner born.

They struck up and Chantal and I took to the floor, followed by everyone else. Even Margot was being guided sedately round by the mayor. She had offered to be in charge of the children while we had a short honeymoon, she was loud in her insistence, and I had booked a weekend at the hotel where Chantal and I had had dinner.

We had a lovely time there, too short, but she had promised to come to Kent soon, when we would have a longer honeymoon in London, which strangely enough she had never seen.

Too soon we were packing up to return to Paris and England, and while we agreed it was a peculiar kind of marriage, we knew it was the best we could do under the circumstances.

'At least it's exciting,' Chantal said. 'I must be the first woman to look forward to her fortieth birthday.'

At Easter, when the children were on holiday from school, Chantal, Mathius and Lenore came to Kent. The reunion was joyful, and we spent some happy days in London, doing the sights. My little cottage was greatly liked, also the village, and none of the Giberts could understand why I preferred Bernay. Nor could I. I wondered if it was because my life seemed to have divided into two parts, England and Merle, and Chantal and Bernay. In any case, we decided to keep the Kent cottage. University careers loomed, and a pied-à-terre near London would be useful for the children, and also for my occasional visits to my agent. Chantal would keep her Marais *appartement* until she retired, then we looked forward to living together at Bernay and welcoming the children when they were free to come.

In June of that year I had to go to Paris, à propos my book on Agnès Sorel, and I thought I'd give her a surprise and call to see her. She was delighted, but she was in the middle of an important case, and explained that she would be busy during the day. Tomorrow she had to be in court, and she suggested I wandered about the Marais. 'When you get to know it, you'll know Paris,' she said. The invidious thought crossed my mind that this marriage was very different from being with Merle, who always had been available for me, then I chided myself, and said, 'OK, that's what I'll do. I'll take you out to dinner tonight, and then I'll set off the following morning.'

She looked at me quizzically. 'You are not disappointed, Martin?' I assured her I wasn't, and set off for my tour round the Marais. It was when I was standing on the Louis-Phillippe bridge and looking down on the river, that I remembered Merle on le Pont Valentré at Cahors.

No looking back, I told myself, Merle is the past, Chantal the future. You are no longer the dominant one in this marriage, Chantal has a life apart from it, and you have to get used to that. You went flying over to Paris, thinking that she would be waiting, ready to fall into your arms. But it is different now. I turned and saw the Pantheon rearing up on the Right Bank, a symbol of Paris, where part of my life would be spent.

As I stood there I felt the familiar frisson that every writer recognizes. The feeling would expand, until the time when it had to be realized on paper. I, too, had a life. I was a writer. I was a happy man.

That evening when we were eating at a bistro in the Village St Paul, Chantal asked me if I had enjoyed my day.

'Immensely,' I said. 'Wonderful background for a future novel. It's Paris, this place, those narrow streets, the gorgeous architecture, those little book shops, it's so French, it's so you!'

'So you're going back to start writing?'

'Yes, and to cure myself from looking backwards, I might write about us, and our family, what's ahead of us . . .'

Her eyes were sparkling. 'Let's play that game. I'll start. What about Betsy?'

I considered. 'I see her as a doctor. She's a bit bossy, but she's got an enquiring mind, and a lot of hidden sweetness.'

'And there's Nick, an enigma? Maybe he will turn out to be a genius.'

I thought of Nick, his tenderness, his aura of being different. 'It wouldn't surprise me. Whatever he turns out to be, I know he'll be a good man. Now Mathius,' I said, 'he's going to be a favourite with all the girls. I watched him at our wedding party dancing with the Vignys' daughter – her arms were round his neck and she was looking up at him and smiling . . .'

'I saw that. What if she were going to have his child and he didn't want to marry her?'

'Chantal!' I felt my eyebrows shoot up. 'What a thought! Maybe you should be a writer. And how do you propose we'd settle that situation . . .?'

'It would be better if there was another suitor in the back-ground, say Guy Rosier's son, who would be willing to marry Yvonne, that's what she's called, and take the baby too.'

'You surprise me,' I said, taking her hand across the table. 'What an imagination!'

'I come across every kind of situation in my work, don't forget.'

'And I just have to imagine them. And how about Lenore?'

'Oh, she's a Parisian, through and through. She'll go to

art school, and after that, she might become a designer of clothes, or of buildings . . .'

'We'll have to remember this conversation. They'll probably surprise us, in any case.'

'Isn't it exciting, though? Will that be your next book?'

'I wouldn't dare. No, it will be set in the Marais, and concerns a beautiful married woman, who fortunately is in love with her husband, and resists all temptation, although she meets many male *avocats* . . .'

'Do you want me to promise?'

'No.' I kissed her hand. 'Promises aren't necessary in a marriage like ours. You're looking,' I said, 'at that rare thing, a happy man.'